JILL FELT AS IF
SHE'D BEEN SLAPPED
IN THE FACE.

She was totally unprepared for the great surge of jealousy that seized her. *Don't be so childish,* she tried to tell herself. *All that was over and finished long ago. It's not as if you've been mooning over Craig for the past few months. You have Jake, and you didn't want to be tied to him anymore. Did you think Craig was going to enter a monastery the moment you two broke up?*

Bantam Books by Janet Quin-Harkin
Ask your bookseller for the books you have missed

On Our Own
BEST
FRIENDS
FOREVER

Janet Quin-Harkin

BANTAM BOOKS
TORONTO · NEW YORK · LONDON · SYDNEY · AUCKLAND

RL 5, IL age 11 and up

BEST FRIENDS FOREVER
A Bantam Book / November 1986

*Sweet Dreams and its associated logo are registered trademarks of
Bantam Books, Inc. Registered in U.S. Patent and Trademark Office
and elsewhere.*

Cover photograph by Pat Hill.

Bantam Books are published by Bantam Books, Inc. Its trademark, consisting of the words "Bantam Books" and the por-
trayal of a rooster, is Registered in U.S. Patent and Trademark
Office and in other countries. Marca Registrada. Bantam
Books, Inc., 666 Fifth Avenue, New York, New York 10103.

PRINTED IN THE UNITED STATES OF AMERICA

O   0 9 8 7 6 5 4 3 2 1

BEST
FRIENDS
FOREVER

ONE

"I must say," Jill Gardner commented as she stood with her best friend, Toni Redmond, outside a door decorated with mock-Grecian columns, "I never thought I would see the day when you went to a fat farm!"

Toni shook back her unruly blond curls and gave Jill one of her famous stares. "It is not a fat farm," she said coldly. "It is a local health spa, right here in Seattle. Lots of people go to health spas who are not fat."

Jill smiled. "I still can't see you bouncing up and down with lots of overweight, middle-aged women in purple leotards."

Toni shrugged her shoulders. "The opportunity was too good to turn down," she said. "It's not every day someone sends you a coupon for a whole month's free use of the spa. I need to get my ankle back in shape after my skiing accident, or I won't be able to take any dance classes. This seems like a good way to do it. I can use their whirlpool and all their equipment."

"It seems too good to be true," Jill said, looking at the fake marble columns. "There must be a catch."

"No catch," Toni said. "They want to introduce sophisticated young career women, like myself, to their facilities."

"Did you mention that you were only a college student?" Jill asked suspiciously.

"I told them I was a secretary," Toni said. "Which I am."

"Only part time," Jill said. "And you're not making enough to pay these prices. I bet they'll come on really strong with a sales pitch to buy a year's membership after your free month."

Toni shrugged again. "I'm a mature adult," she said. "I know high-pressure sales tactics. Remember how I managed to pressure all those artists into coming to the theater's craft fair? I can handle it."

"Are you sure you don't want me to come in with you?" Jill looked down anxiously at her friend. Toni was wearing bright red painters' overalls and a red- and white-striped sweatshirt, and her hair was caught up on one side in a bright red bow. As usual she had on very little makeup.

She had been living in her own apartment and managing a job at the Theater Alliance for several months, but she still managed to look like an orphan in need of protection.

Toni shook her head firmly. "I'm a big girl, Jill. I can handle it myself. You go browse in the bookstore, and I'll meet you out here in an hour, okay?"

Jill couldn't resist a glance back as Toni disappeared through the double glass doors and down the thickly carpeted mirror-lined hallway. Now that Jill was away most of the time, at Rosemont College in Oregon, she knew that Toni could survive perfectly well without her. She also knew that Toni, in a matter of moments, could turn an ordinary situation into an extraordinary one.

Only three weeks before, Toni, who was only a novice skier, had tried out for a skiing role in a movie. In the middle of a steep, dangerous run, she had careened out of control and sailed over the heads of the camera crew. She had escaped with only a sprained ankle and some bruises. In spite of her antics, Toni seemed to lead a charmed life.

At least interesting things happen to me when I'm with her, Jill decided as she crossed the street and pushed open the door to a favorite bookstore.

Toni was leaning casually against one of the

marble pillars in front of the health club when Jill returned for her an hour later.

"You look very fresh and relaxed," Jill said. "I thought people crawled out of places like this dripping with sweat."

"Only those who are out of shape," Toni said, falling into step beside her friend as they walked down the block toward the parking lot.

"So how was it?" Jill asked. "Did you have to go through the big sales pitch and sign up for twenty years of membership?"

"Nope," Toni said. "Nobody pressured me at all."

"Amazing," Jill said. "You mean they just welcomed you for one month and didn't try to get you to buy a membership?"

"Yep," Toni said.

"I can't believe it," Jill commented. They walked for a while in silence, their two pairs of shoes tapping in unison on the sidewalk.

"Of course," Toni finally said, "my encounter with the machine might have had something to do with it."

"What machine?" Jill asked suspiciously.

A grin flickered across Toni's face. "You know what I'm like with machines," she said.

"I know exactly what you are like with machines," Jill said dryly. "What happened with this one?"

The grin spread across Toni's face. "I acciden-

4

tally leaned on the switch," she said. "I mean, what a stupid place to put it, on a thing that looked like an armrest. I was just resting my arm, looking around for what to do first, and I switched it on by mistake."

"What happened to you?" Jill asked. "Did you hurt yourself?"

"Nothing happened to *me*," Toni said calmly. "It was the woman who was standing on the machine, getting ready to use it, who was surprised." Toni's whole face lit up at the memory of it. "You would have died, Jill. She was bending over, tying her aerobic shoe, and suddenly the machine came on. It was a hip vibrator. She was super fat to start with, and she was wearing this purple and orange outfit. Suddenly the whole machine started vibrating. She tried to stand up, but this vibrating belt had her imprisoned. It was so-o-o funny."

"I take it the woman didn't think so?" Jill asked, smiling.

The grin faded from Toni's face. "You should have heard her scream! No wonder opera singers are all fat," she said. "The panic she caused—people started running in all directions. I tried to tell them it was an accident but I don't think they believed me. Anyway, some woman guarded me the rest of the time, and they didn't ask me to become a member."

"So, are you going for the rest of your month?" Jill asked.

Toni shook her head. "I don't think so," she said. "What would I want from a fat farm?"

Jill opened the car door. "Now you know why I hate to leave you and go back to college," she said as she leaned to open Toni's door. "One hour without me and you can wreck the most durable establishment. I'm beginning to think I'd better not go back tomorrow."

"I wish you weren't going back," Toni said. "I just got used to having you around again. I'm going to miss you."

Jill smiled. "Only until Brandt gets back," she said. "After that you wouldn't notice if I was here or not."

"That's not true," Toni said. "It's wonderful having Brandt around, but I still miss you. After all, he hasn't known me since I was seven. You and I know everything about each other, Jill. We've suffered through each other's chicken pox and tonsils and broken hearts. I can tell you all my crazy fears and dreams, just as if I were talking to a mirror."

"I know how you feel, Toni," Jill said quietly. "Because I feel the same way. I really wish you were at Rosemont with me."

"Now that's something I do not wish!" Toni said firmly. "The thought of having to study morning, noon, and night in that brain factory is

6

not one that appeals to me! All those people wanting to discuss Chaucer and Einstein in their spare time!"

Jill smiled. "Jake does not want to discuss Einstein in his spare time, as you very well remember."

Toni shot Jill a wicked look. "Jake is a normal male, I must agree. If I didn't have Brandt around I would envy you, going back to him. But I still wouldn't look forward to a whole semester of study, study, study."

"I'm really looking forward to going back," Jill said. "It's hard work for me, but I feel great when a professor says I've made a good point or written a good paper. The only thing I'm not looking forward to is the science class I've got to take this semester for my breadth requirement."

"Your what?" Toni asked. "You have to measure a perfect thirty-four, twenty-four, thirty-six or something?"

Jill giggled. "You are funny sometimes. The breadth requirement means that if you're an arts major, you have to take a certain number of science courses, and if you're a science major, you have to do some arts. To stop you from graduating as a boring person, I guess."

Toni wrinkled her nose. "I'd rather graduate as a boring person," she said. "Business math was enough for me. From now on it's going to be only dance and drama."

"Well, of course, that makes sense for you, because that's what you want to do with your life," Jill said. "But most people don't know exactly what they want to do, so it's not too wise to specialize."

"Hey, what a great title for a song," Toni interrupted. "It's not too wise, to specialize," she crooned, beating out a rhythm on the dashboard. She looked across at Jill and grinned sheepishly. "It's a good thing it's you going to Rosemont and not me," she said. "I'd turn every professor's hair gray overnight."

"All the same," Jill said, "I often wish you were around to cheer me up. I get so serious sometimes. I start worrying about all my assignments and the newspaper and the magazine. I need someone like you to start acting crazy and remind me that life is meant to be fun. Even Jake will be working hard this semester, because he graduates in the spring. I don't know what I'll do next year with no Jake."

"You're thinking long-term relationship?" Toni asked, raising an eyebrow.

Jill felt herself flushing slightly. "I don't know," she said. "And I don't know how long he'll want to be tied to one girl, but I do know that right now the future would be bleak without him."

"I know the feeling," Toni said. "I just can't think of life without Brandt. Every time I daydream about my future, he's included. Even when I'm a big star in Hollywood, I see him there directing my picture!"

"What I like about you, Toni Redmond," Jill said, "is that your plans are not humble. My only wish for the future is to get through the next semester with passing grades."

"That's why you need me as a friend," Toni said. "My cheerful, optimistic, sunny personality keeps you going!"

The car swung onto Jill's street. "You want to come in for some brownies?" Jill asked. "Or do you want me to drop you off with your folks?"

"Brownies?" Toni's eyes lit up. "Your mother has been making brownies?"

Jill nodded. "I think she was overcome with guilt about neglecting her daughter all vacation, so she took a couple of days off from work. She needed them, too. She'd been working so hard before Christmas. They had this brief to prepare for a big court case—"

"Someone was suing Santa Claus because his reindeer knocked down a chimney?" Toni quipped.

"Much more boring than that," Jill said. "Some sort of compensation case—"

"Santa was suing because he slipped off the roof?"

"Oh, shut up," Jill said, laughing. "Anyway, she's taking a few days off before I go back to

9

college and baking all my favorite things. It's just like the old times, only it will make it harder not to feel homesick back at school."

"I'd willingly suffer pangs of homesickness for a few of your mother's brownies," Toni said, leaping out of the car. "Come on, last one in is a rotten egg!"

And she sprinted down the front path, leaving Jill shaking her head in amusement. "I don't think you'll ever grow up, Toni Redmond," Jill muttered to herself as she caught up with Toni.

TWO

January 15

This is the fifth diary my grandmother in Chicago has sent me. This year I'm really going to keep it up. I'm already past January 10, which is a record. Also I'm not going to write down boring stuff like "went to school." "Did homework." "Had fried chicken for dinner." "Saw a cute boy." I'm really going to pour my heart out to this diary. That way, when I'm famous, I can have it published and get on the best-seller list. I'm sure everyone will want to read about the agony I went through, struggling to the top!

Jill goes back to college tomorrow. I'll miss her. We were together long enough this time to become best friends again. I've just gotten used to being able to call her every time I want to tell her something, and tomorrow she'll be far away again. Sometimes I wish everything had gone as we planned it, and we were both at State U. But then I wouldn't have had the lead in a play, or a real job, or met Brandt—and I can't imagine life without him. He comes back again day after tomorrow! I'm counting the minutes. I guess it really must be love this time. I've had lots of boyfriends, and some of them were very cute, but I've never had a boyfriend who crept into my thoughts all the time. We've been going together for about three months now, and my heart still beats fast every time I think about him. Hurry up and get back here, Brandt. *I miss you, miss you, miss you.*

Good night, dear diary. I've got to get my beauty sleep because my dance classes start this week. I really want to be a star in them. I want everyone else to stop dancing and watch me as the teacher says, "Why haven't you been discovered before? Watching you is watching poetry in motion."

Of course, the last time I took dance classes, at Miss Marvel's, I got thrown out for kicking a little girl with my tap shoes on. She deserved it—she laughed at me because I couldn't get the time step right. Anyway, this will be different. I promise not to kick anybody, and I intend to get all the steps right, immediately, even if I have to stay up all night practicing. Oh dear, I wonder if my landlord will mind my doing leaps across his ceiling all night?

My thoughts are getting muddled— somebody will have to edit this before it makes the best-seller list. What I'm trying to say, I think, is that I am determined to do something well, and I think I can do really well at dance and drama. I want to show Jill she's not the only one in the world with talent.

Sleet spattered across the windshield and bare branches rattled and shivered as Mr. Gardner swung the big car in through the gates of Rosemont College. Some of the older, traditional buildings covered in naked ivy vines looked grim and forbidding after the long ride up the rhodo-dendron-lined drive.

"What a terrible day," Mrs. Gardner said. "I'm glad the campus looked more friendly the first time we came last fall, Jill. Right now it looks like a set from a horror movie."

"But it's really cozy inside, Mom," Jill said. "It's warm and cozy in McGregor, my dorm. Cassandra and I can lie in our beds on rainy nights and listen to the rain drumming on the porch roof. It makes you feel very snug."

"Your mother and I really wanted to treat you to a last good dinner this evening, Jill," Mr.

Gardner said. "Are you sure you don't want to change your mind and take us up on that?"

"Quite sure. Thanks, Dad," Jill said. "I know college food isn't the greatest, but everyone will be in the cafeteria tonight, swapping winter-break stories. I don't want to miss out on anything. Besides, I'm dying to see them all again. And I know you'd like to drive home before it gets dark."

"I must admit that I'm not too happy about driving more than a hundred and fifty miles in the dark and rain," her father said. "And your mother worries—"

"So you two drop me off and drive straight home," Jill said, patting her father on his shoulder as he drove. "I'll be just fine."

Jill's mother looked at her and smiled. "Who would know it was only a little more than four months ago that we drove you up this same driveway for the first time—"

"I was scared silly," Jill interrupted.

"Were you?" her mother asked, looking surprised.

"Petrified," Jill confessed. "I thought everyone else would be rich and supersmart and I'd never have the courage to talk to anyone, let alone make any friends."

"You were a good actress, then," her mother said, smiling back at her. "You seemed very cool

14

and composed. I thought I was the only one who was going to cry."

"I was fighting off tears all afternoon," Jill said. "I didn't want you to see me looking unhappy, but a few tears did squeeze out the moment you left."

"And this time you can't wait to get rid of us," Mr. Gardner said heartily.

"Daddy!" Jill exclaimed in a shocked voice. "You know that's not true. It was wonderful being home again, even if it was only for a couple of weeks. Even mature adult college students enjoy eating homemade brownies and going to sleep with their stuffed animals around them!"

Jill's parents both laughed, and Jill peered ahead between them, trying to catch the first glimpse of her dorm as they turned the corner at the administration building. "Although I must admit," she said as they turned toward the back of the campus, "I can hardly wait to see everyone again. I've got so much to tell Cassie, and I've got to find out which courses all my friends have signed up for."

"And you've got to start training for water polo again." Mr. Gardner chuckled.

"Water polo was a fall sport," Jill reminded him. "No more polo until next fall, thank heavens. I couldn't keep up that training much longer. I would have turned into a beefy superjock."

"I wish we'd had a chance to see you in a game," Mr. Gardner said wistfully.

"I'm glad you didn't," Jill said. "I only played in one game, but it wasn't a pretty sight. When I finally did get the ball some huge guy from the other team nearly drowned me. You'd have been worried sick and ready to dive in after me."

"I most certainly would have," her mother said. "Wasn't there somebody to stop those bullies from pushing you under the water?"

Jill laughed. "It's part of the game, Mom. You try to foul the person with the ball, because then they have to pass and not take a shot at the goal. You can do what you like as long as you go for the ball and not the person."

Mrs. Gardner looked shocked. "I had no idea my daughter was involved in such a rough sport," she said.

"But it was fun, Mom," Jill said, patting her arm. "I really liked it, especially after I learned the rules and knew what I was doing. For the first couple weeks of practice people kept yelling, 'sluff, sluff,' at me, and I thought they were saying, 'smurf.' I made the whole team crack up when I asked the coach what smurf meant."

"Here we are, safe and sound," Jill's father said, drawing to a halt outside the white wooden house with its gabled roof and long porch. "We're going to get drenched carrying your stuff in."

"It's okay, Dad," Jill said. "I'll go inside and

try to find somebody to help me carry. You and Mom stay dry. I bet lots of my friends are already here."

Before she could even open the car door, however, a window was thrown up in the corner room, and a small white face surrounded by masses of long black hair looked out, saw the car and broke into frantic waves. She turned from the window and seconds later appeared at the front door, rushing down the steps toward the car, a beaded black shawl streaming out behind her and her hair blown across her face.

"Jill," she yelled, fighting to push her hair free of her mouth.

"Cassie!" Jill screamed, leaping out of the car. They rushed toward each other.

"You two girls will catch pneumonia if you stand around there," Mr. Gardner shouted from the car as the two girls hugged and danced on the sidewalk. "Go do your hugging inside, then come back out with your raincoats on," he yelled.

Jill looked up, her hair already plastered to her face. "Oh, Dad, we're fine," she cried. "I'm a tough water polo player now, you know."

"Besides," Cassie added, "we have to walk across to the cafeteria in all kinds of weather. We'll survive a few drops of rain."

"Looks like more than a few drops to me," Mr. Gardner said, leaning back into the car. "But then maybe I'm getting old."

"So, how was your vacation?" Cassandra asked Jill, throwing the shawl back over her shoulder as she grabbed a bag from the trunk of the car.

"Wonderful," Jill said. "I've got so much to tell you, Cassie."

"And I've got so much to tell you," Cassandra said. "I had a fantastic vacation, too."

"Where did you go?" Jill demanded, staggering up the steps under the weight of a huge suitcase. "I tried calling your house when I got back from Snowfire, but a maid or someone said you were away."

"I *was* away," Cassandra said, beaming across at Jill. "At the most marvelous place, and I can't wait to tell you all about it."

"Just come inside," Jill called to her father. We'll bring in the rest of the stuff in a minute." She kicked open the front door and looked around in satisfaction. "It smells just the same," she said.

Cassandra looked surprised. "You didn't think they'd redecorate over vacation, did you?"

Jill laughed. "No, silly. I just meant it felt good to be back and that I'd missed it. Is our room just the same?"

"No—they put in a huge water bed and a mirror on the ceiling and shrunken heads around the walls," Cassandra said over her shoulder as they walked to the room. "No—just kidding, it's exactly the same."

Jill pushed open their door. The room looked just as she remembered it—same faded rose pink drapes and rugs, same heavy mahogany furniture, and a large black and white cat curled up in the middle of her bed. "Oh, Jelly Bean," she called, rushing over to pick up the cat. Jelly Bean half opened her eyes and started purring like a motor.

"Is everyone else back?" Jill asked, putting down the cat and shaking the rain out of her hair.

"There has been a constant procession in here all afternoon," Cassandra said, dumping Jill's heavy case on the floor and taking off her sodden shawl. "Every two minutes a head poked around the door and someone asked, 'Is Jill back yet?' I felt like an answering service."

"Did a certain someone poke his head 'round the door yet?" Jill asked.

Cassandra raised an eyebrow. "So that's still on, is it? No, he hasn't put in an appearance yet, but I expect he's waiting for a grand entrance tonight. Terrence dropped by, though—took one look at me and fled. I think he's still convinced I'm a witch."

Jill's parents carried the last of the things from the car: homemade cookies, a box of instant hot chocolate with marshmallows, and a crate full of books.

"If you keep bringing back more and more stuff each vacation, you're going to need a whole floor of rooms to yourself by the time you're a senior," her mother commented. "This room is bulging at the seams already."

"You should have seen what Sheridan brought," Jill commented. Sheridan, her first roommate, had seemed to own every electrical appliance, plus three full wardrobes of clothes. "Cassie and I have very simple tastes compared to most college students."

"Except for books," Cassandra reminded her. "We do have more than our share of books. I brought a whole lot more back with me, too, but I bought one of those revolving book racks from a bookstore. We can store all our paperbacks in the corner."

"What a super idea," Jill said. "That will give us a lot more space. Let's get started putting them in now."

"I can see you don't need us around here anymore," Jill's father said. "So I think we'll be getting back."

Jill looked up guiltily. "Oh, Dad, wouldn't you like me to make you a cup of coffee or something first?" she asked. "You've got such a long drive ahead of you."

"It's okay, darling, we'll stop on the way

home," her mother said. "I can tell you're dying to be with your friends again. And your father is anxious to get going." She went across to Jill and put her arms around her. "Have a good semester, darling, won't you? We're so happy to see you fitting in so well here." She kissed Jill and then turned away quickly. "Come on, Arthur. Long drive ahead," she said in a clipped voice.

"Goodbye, Jill," her father said solemnly, wrapping her into a bear hug. "Take care of yourself. And write to let your mother know what you're doing. She worries about you. . . ." Then he turned and followed his wife down the hall.

Jill watched them go. "I feel guilty, Cassie," she said. "They were almost in tears, and I couldn't wait to get back here. I really don't feel homesick at all. I loved being home, of course, and I loved seeing them again, but I felt as if I didn't really belong at home anymore. I kept thinking about Rosemont and all my friends."

Cassandra nodded. "Don't forget that you were like an only child. Your sister had her own life for a long time, and, of course, your parents will miss you. Also it hurts them to see you so independent and grown-up. It reminds them that you don't really need them anymore."

"That's why I'm so glad my mother has her job now," Jill said. "She's enjoying it so much, and people are relying on her more and more at the office, so she feels needed there." She squatted down beside her case and began unpacking. "But it's not true that I don't need them anymore," she said thoughtfully. "When I was sick last semester, the first person I wanted was my mommy. I don't think I'll ever be able to do without them. It's hard. Don't you feel it's like stepping into a time warp to go home and then come back?"

Cassandra nodded thoughtfully. "Only my time warp is usually a horror episode," she said. "I count the days until I'm out of my house."

"Was it just as bad this time?" Jill asked.

"Worse," Cassandra said. "My mother planned this huge Christmas party, which was funny because most of their friends are Jewish—but she didn't care about that. It was an opportunity for her to show off the hugest Christmas tree in town and her new silver dress. She wanted to show me off, too, and team me up with some nice doctor's son, I think. But I escaped. I spent a dreamy vacation—"

"Where did you go?" Jill demanded.

"The Marine Wildlife Center on the coast," Cassandra said, a faraway look in her eyes. "It was heaven! Three weeks of climbing into tide pools and observing sea lions and whales. What more could anyone ask?"

Jill shook her head. "It doesn't sound like my dream vacation, Cassie," she said. "Why don't you tell me about it while I get unpacked?"

THREE

Jill had hardly had time to unpack the first layer from her suitcase when there was a thunderous pounding on the door, and Marcie, an upperclassman from across the hall, poked her head in.

"See, I told you they were back," she shouted to unseen people. Without waiting for an invitation, a group swarmed into the room.

"Well, we're all together again, which must mean that we all passed our finals last semester," Marcie commented when the noise died down.

"I couldn't believe it when I got my grades," Jill said. "I was so happy. It made my vacation. I'd really been worried."

"As if you had anything to worry about," Heather, Marcie's roommate, commented. "I can tell a born brain when I see one. I bet you got all A's."

"Not even close," Jill said, turning pink. She had gotten an A on her English exam, thanks to Jake's coaching. "But at least we all passed, which is great."

"Did you guys have a good vacation?" Marcie asked.

"I had a wonderful time at the marine research station at the Wildlife Center," Cassandra said, the faraway look coming into her eyes again. "They are discovering such fascinating things about starfish."

Jill saw a look pass between two of the other girls.

"What about you, Jill?" Marcie asked quietly. "Did you get away, or were you stuck at home?"

"I worked at a new ski resort," Jill said. "It was hard work, but lots of fun. My best friend was up there with me."

"So you didn't see Jake?" Marcie asked, settling herself down amid the clutter on Jill's bed and pushing Jelly Bean out of the way. "I heard he was going up to his family's cabin."

"Actually he changed his mind and came up to the ski resort with me," Jill said, trying to stop herself from blushing furiously as she spoke. She was conscious of several pairs of eyes regarding her with interest.

"Wow, how about that?" Heather said. "A whole vacation with Jake Randall."

"It wasn't a whole vacation," Jill said hastily. "I spent some of the time with my folks, too, and Jake had to visit his parents."

"I wouldn't say no to even one week with Jake Randall," Heather said, grinning. "That sounds like my kind of vacation."

Jill felt as if she would squirm with embarrassment, so she rapidly changed the subject. "How about some hot chocolate, you guys?" she asked. "I brought this giant box back with me, complete with marshmallows."

"Terrific," Marcie said.

"I'll put the water on," Cassandra said, getting up from her seat. Jill watched her go. *Poor Cassie doesn't feel at ease with people like this*, she thought. *She always manages to say the wrong thing. I have to do something this semester to help her*.

"So what about your vacation, Marcie," Jill asked. "Did you get away in the end, or were you stuck with your little brother?"

Marcie made a face. "Nonstop baby-sitting. Seven-year-old boys are totally disgusting. They make noises all the time and run racing cars up and down your back. How they ever grow up to become hunks I don't know."

There was another knock on the door, and someone called, "Is Jill there yet?" Then Jason's head appeared. He looked around the room, said, "Oh, good, a party," and came inside.

"Robert's been looking for you all afternoon," he commented.

"Gee, you are popular," Heather said, shaking her head. "Why don't boys keep hammering on my door all day?"

Jill got up and began handing out cups of hot chocolate. "It's not like that," she said. "Robert and Jason were some of the first friends we made here, right, Cassie?"

"You mean Sheridan wasn't your first friend?" Cassie asked Jill, with a sideways grin.

"Very funny," Jill said, remembering the way she had clashed with her first roommate and how she had despaired of ever meeting people who were like her. Now there she was with a whole roomful of people sitting comfortably around her and talking like old friends. She looked around, satisfied.

Cassandra glanced out of the window. "Uh, oh. Here comes Terrence," she said.

Jill turned pale. "Oh, I don't know if I want to face him yet," she said.

"What's wrong with Terrence?" Heather demanded. "I think he's cute."

"He's really nice," Jill said. "There's nothing wrong with him. He's a very nice person."

"Except that he followed Jill around like a

26

faithful hound all last semester," Cassie interrupted.

"But I thought you liked him?" Heather asked, puzzled.

Jill pushed back her hair in embarrassment. "I did like him, but that was all. I wasn't in love with him."

"And he got really mad at Jill when she started going with Jake," Cassandra added.

"Let's forget about it," Jill said uneasily. "I don't like talking about people behind their backs—"

She broke off as a timid tap sounded at the door. Terrence came in, saw the room full of people, and hesitated.

"Come on in, you're just in time for hot chocolate," Jill said, smiling at him encouragingly.

"Well, if you're sure," he said, looking around before perching himself on the edge of the desk.

"Sorry about the mess," Jill apologized. "People started coming in as soon as I got here."

"It's been like a royal court all afternoon," Cassie commented, handing Terrence a steaming mug. "I feel like a lady-in-waiting to the queen. Yes, her majesty is in residence. Do you require an audience?"

Everyone laughed. Jill waited until the group

had broken into noisy chatter before she walked across to Terrence. "Did you have a good vacation?" she asked cautiously.

He nodded. "It was fine," he said. "It did me good to get away for a while. I think I'd been pushing myself too hard at college last semester. Everything seemed to be getting on top of me. So I lazed around doing nothing and eating a lot. Now I feel a lot better." He looked at her steadily. "I think I've got my head together again."

"And your heart?" Jill asked, smiling at him gently.

"That, too," he said. "I dated an old friend from school in the vacation. Nothing serious, but it was fun."

"I'm glad."

He continued to look at her seriously. "How about you and what's-his-name?" he asked.

"Jake and I had a great vacation together," she said. "Does that answer your question?"

Terrence nodded. "Don't worry, Jill. Just friends from now on, okay?"

Jill reached out and laid her hand on his. "You've always been my friend, Terrence," she said.

"So what science class are you going to take?" he asked Jill, changing the subject.

"I don't know yet," she said. "The easiest one, I hope."

"I think I'll take the history of science and

technology," Terrence said. "That way I don't have to cut up horrible squirmy things in labs."

"That's not a bad idea," Jill said. "Maybe I'll take it with you."

"Oh, but you can't," Cassandra blurted out. "I want you to take marine biology with me, Jill. It's such a wonderful course. We'll go on a few Saturdays for field trips to the research station and spend a whole week there in February. You should have seen the baby sea lions, Jill. And when we went out whale watching, whole groups of dolphins swam around the boat. It's heavenly. I know you'd love it."

"I don't know, Cassie," Jill said hesitantly. "I'll think about it, okay?"

"Maybe I'll take it, too," Terrence said.

"I'll bug you both until you give in," Cassandra said. "Oh, look, there's Robert." Robert came in, dripping from the rain and pink cheeked from the wind. He grinned when he saw Jill. "I've been looking for you," he said.

"You want to come to pay homage at the queen's court?" Cassandra asked dryly.

Robert laughed. "No way. I've come to drag her off to work."

"Work, already?" Jill asked, horrified.

Robert produced some papers from under his jacket and waved them in her face. "Literary magazine, dear coeditor. Need I remind you that we didn't finish the winter edition before vacation? When I got here this morning, I had some senior on my back, wanting to know when the magazine was coming out. I didn't tell him that we have a grand total of three pages of poems."

"Oh, yes," Jill said. "I forgot all about the magazine. I guess we'd better start working soon."

"We'd better get busy writing poems right away," Robert said. "I can't stretch the few we have into a magazine. Nobody in his right mind would pay a dollar for a couple pages of poetry. Any of you guys feel creative?"

Marcie got up with a horrified look. "Count me out," she said. "We chemistry majors can't string more than two words of English together— this is a well-known fact. Besides, I've got to get unpacked before dinner. Coming, Heather?" She made a hasty exit, followed by Heather and the other girls.

Robert looked from Jill to Cassandra, Jason, and Terrence. "Isn't it amazing how the simple word 'poem' can clear a room in seconds?" he commented. "It can't be that hard to write a poem, can it?"

Jill looked at him thoughtfully. "Poetry is so personal to some people," she said. "It's like putting your soul on a piece of paper for all the world to see."

"I didn't say they had to be deep poems," Robert said, sighing. "Even a simple limerick would do. You're an English major, Terrence, what about you?"

"I've already written one," Terrence said. "But I might manage a couple more, I suppose."

"Cassie writes poetry," Jill said, turning to her roommate. "How about it?"

Cassie shrugged her shoulders. "I'll write you a poem if you'll agree to take marine biology this semester," she said.

Jill laughed. "That's blackmail," she said.

"All right," Cassie said. "I'll write you two poems if you'll join marine biology."

"You're terrible, Cassie," she said. "But if you want me to do it that much, I suppose I could. Only you're going to have to cut up starfish and sea worms for me. I can't do stuff like that."

"I'll do the dissections," Cassie said. "I just want you to share the excitement, Jill."

"I'm not so sure about that," Jill said. "But I'm desperate for poems right now."

"You could always ask Jake for a few more," Terrence commented. "He's so creative he could toss them off the top of his head."

"She doesn't have time to talk about poetry when she's with Jake," Cassie said wickedly. Jill shot her a frown.

"That's a good idea, Terrence," Jill said. "Jake knows all the seniors, anyway. He can ask other people to write some. He's already contributed some." She looked around the room. "Now, if you guys don't mind," she said, "I haven't even had a chance to unpack yet. Why don't you let me get the room in order, and we'll meet you at dinner."

"I get the hint we're not wanted," Jason said to Robert, standing up.

"Unless you want to load three thousand books into a rack," Jill said sweetly.

"I think we'll leave you and let you unpack," Robert said, grinning. "We'd only take up space. Come on, Terrence."

The three boys trooped out. Jill shut the door with a sigh. "*Phew*. College is a little overpowering when you've been used to the quiet of home, isn't it?" she asked. "Everyone talks at once."

"Well, at least the queen has now dismissed her faithful followers," Cassandra said.

Jill came over to her. "Does it bug you to have everyone dropping in like that?" she asked. "I wasn't really acting like a queen at a royal court, was I?"

Cassandra laughed. "Of course not. I was only teasing. Large crowds of noisy people are not my thing, exactly, but only because I don't feel easy with people like Marcie. I know she thinks I'm weird, and so does Heather, just because I'd rather talk about starfish than boys."

"You should have said something," Jill told her friend, "I'd have kicked them out if I'd known they were upsetting you."

"Don't be dumb," Cassandra said. "It's your room, too. You have every right to have friends dropping in, and I don't really mind them. It's kind of fun playing lady-in-waiting!"

At that moment there was a discreet tap on the door, and a deep voice called in, "Anybody home?"

Cassie looked up at Jill, who had leaped toward the door.

"I think this is the moment for the lady-in-waiting to take the cups down to the kitchen and wash them," she said, scooping together the mugs onto a tray.

Jill beamed. "Cassie, you're a good friend," she said. "I'll do the same for you one day."

"Let's hope it's one day soon," Cassandra said as Jill opened the door to let Jake in. She quickly slipped past him.

"I've missed you terribly," he complained as he wrapped Jill in his arms. "You have no idea how boring it was at home without you!"

Jill laughed. "But we were only apart for a couple of weeks."

Jake looked hurt. "You mean you didn't miss me?"

"Of course, I missed you," Jill said. "But I had so much to do at home that the days just flew by. My mother took some time off from work and we went out a lot. It was really great to have my mom and Toni around."

"Lucky you," Jake said. "I had my mother around, too, but I can't say the experience was too wonderful. She did nothing but cross-examine me about my father and his new wife."

Jill slid her arms around Jake's neck. "Poor Jake," she said. "I'm sorry your vacation was such a bummer. Next vacation you can come to my house. My mother will take one look at you and decide you're undernourished and start making hearty soups for you!"

Jake laughed. "You'd better tell her I have an appetite like a horse. I'm just one of those people who doesn't put on weight. My creative genius eats up the calories!"

"Oh, speaking of creative genius," Jill said, "I have a big favor to ask you."

"Anything for you," he whispered, kissing her gently on the tip of her nose.

"I need some more poems for the winter edition of the literary magazine," Jill said. "I thought you could persuade some of your senior friends to write us some. I'd ask you to write more, but you've already given us the best ones we've got."

Jake smiled. "You sure know how to flatter a guy," he said. "I'll see what I can do for you."

"Thank you, you're terrific. Did I ever tell you that?" she asked, gazing up at him adoringly.

"Yes, but tell me again," he said, his eyes teasing.

"Okay," Jill whispered. "You are one terrific guy, and I'm very lucky to have you around."

"You know, it's really good to be appreciated," Jake said. "Now would you mind answering one question for me? Why are we having this long conversation when your roommate is out of the room, we haven't seen each other in a while, and we're all alone?"

Jill stood on tiptoe to bring her lips to his. "The conversation has ended," she whispered.

FOUR

"I can't believe it," Jill said, gazing up at Jake delightedly. "I don't know how you managed to do it, but you've saved us from looking like complete fools."

"It wasn't too hard," Jake said, shrugging his shoulders. "You just have to know the right people."

"But twenty poems in two days!" Jill said. "Robert will go crazy. Now we can actually get the winter edition out before all the tree buds start bursting." She glanced down at the sheaf of papers in her hands. "Hey, some of these are good, too."

"I told you I knew the right people," Jake said. "And it was much easier to persuade them when I told them they could submit their poems anonymously."

"I wish more of them had signed their names," Jill said. "Now I'll stare at every member of the senior class wondering who wrote what."

"I'll never tell," Jake said. "My lips are sealed."

Jill reached out and ran her finger down his cheek. "I have ways to unseal them," she said. Jake laughed and slid his arms around her. "Do you know how the time dragged without you?" he asked. "I kept looking at the calendar and saying, 'It can't only be Wednesday!'"

"I had so much to do that I hardly had the time to miss you," Jill confessed. "You know what Toni can be like—she dragged me from one thing to the next, including a ladies' health spa, which I must tell you about in grim detail sometime."

Jake chuckled. "I can imagine," he said, "having seen the most spectacular ski accident ever witnessed. How is her ankle, by the way?"

"Fine," Jill said. "She's been going to physical therapy, and her doctor says she can start dance classes when her semester begins this week. She's going to concentrate on dance and drama from now on, which makes sense, since that's what she wants to do. No more computers and business math."

Jake shook his head. "She's quite a girl," he said. "I really enjoyed having her around." He looked down at Jill, his eyes serious for a moment. "Of course, I would have enjoyed it more if you and I had been all alone."

"Hmmm," Jill said doubtfully. "And I would have spent the whole time fighting you off!"

"Wrong," he said good-naturedly. "With nobody else around, my natural charm and persuasive patter would immediately have convinced you that you were wasting your time resisting me."

Jill laughed. "I'll say one thing about you, Jake Randall. Modesty is not one of your strong points." She glanced again at the stack of papers. "But where poetry is concerned, you are a total miracle worker!"

He looked down into her eyes. "There's just one miracle I haven't yet managed to bring off," he said.

"Let's not go over that again," Jill said. "I told you my feelings."

"And you also told me you might change your mind sometime," he said.

"But not if you're going to pressure me," Jill said firmly.

Jake looked hurt. "Who said anything about pressuring? I plan to be my usual, gentlemanly self," he said.

"That's what I'm afraid of," Jill said, smiling up at him.

He pulled her close to him. "You have

nothing to be afraid of, Jill," he whispered, brushing her lips with his.

"I know," she whispered as she brought her lips up to his for a real, lingering kiss.

"This is great! A whole thick book of poetry!" Jill said, waving a sheaf of papers at Robert as he joined her in the union later that morning. "Russel just offered to do the typesetting on the computer for us. I really think we'll have a magazine to be proud of."

Robert nodded. "Not bad, considering neither of us wanted to take over the magazine in the first place."

"I was so worried about this last semester, Robert," she said. "There were times when I didn't think we could do it. It's amazing what difference a vacation can make."

"And how nice it is to start out with all new courses," he added. "I'm glad we don't have to face Western civilization anymore."

"I couldn't wait to get rid of psychology," Jill confessed. "I really thought I'd enjoy it, but I can't go along with the idea that nine-tenths of the world is suffering from some complex. I found myself staring at people in the cafeteria and wondering what phobias they were displaying. At least psychiatry is one profession I can rule out now."

"But you're going back to Dr. Holloman for more English," Robert commented. "I thought you hated him!"

"I don't like him," Jill said. "As a person, that is. He still terrifies me, and he has no consideration for other people's feelings. But he is a terrific teacher; you can't deny that. I felt I really knew how to put together a good paper by the end of that class. And I did get an A on my final, so he must like my work."

"Well, of course, if you're a brain, that's different," Robert said. "But for us humble B's—"

"I did have some help with the final," Jill confessed. "Jake told me what sorts of questions he always asks and who his favorite authors are, so I studied heavily on those. Jake's one of those lucky people who seems to have a feel for exams. He always breezes through with A's and does no work at all."

Robert looked at her steadily. "Did it ever occur to you that he just breezes through because he's brilliant?" he asked.

"Oh, I'm sure he's pretty smart," Jill said.

"Brilliant," Robert corrected. "Maybe even a genius."

"Oh, come on." Jill laughed uneasily. "I can't see myself dating a genius."

"What else would you call a person who

wrote twenty good poems in two days?" Robert asked.

Jill looked at him suspiciously. "What are you talking about?" she demanded. "He got other seniors to write those poems."

Robert shook his head.

"He didn't?" Jill wavered.

"I went up to Russel and congratulated him on his beautiful poem," Robert said. "And he didn't know what I was talking about. I felt like a fool. Russel and Jake used to room together, so I guess Jake thought he could use Russel's name."

"But why would Jake do that?" Jill asked, feeling confused.

"Simple. He knows we can't have twenty poems by one person in the magazine, so he pretends they're poems by twenty different people. That way he saves our magazine and doesn't have to go to the trouble of asking other people to write for him. You know Jake is basically lazy."

Jill shook her head and gave an uneasy laugh. "You're right," she said. "What a crazy thing to do. I bet he was going to tell Russel about it, and he just didn't get around to it. What do we do now, Robert?"

Robert's eyes opened wide in surprise. "Use the poems, of course. Are you crazy? They're the best stuff we've got."

Jill started to laugh. "He's crazy! Just wait until I get him!"

"He must care a lot about you, to go to all that trouble," Robert commented. "Could you write twenty poems, just like that?"

Jill picked up the papers. "I have to read them all again. I just glanced through them before. I was so glad to get those extra pages that I would have printed cooking recipes. But now I want to read them."

"They're all good and all different," Robert said. "He can just write in any style he chooses. Stick with him, Jill. He's probably going to make millions as a screenwriter one day."

Jill continued to flick through the pages. "Did I tell you, Cassie turned in her poems, too," she said. "'Starfish brittle-armed, sun-dappled . . .' Hey, this one is good!"

"You should read her other one carefully, it's even better," Robert said. "Different and better."

Jill took out another page with Cassandra's name on it.

"'Merman?'" she asked, reading the title.

I saw you on the shoreline, half in spray,
The wind was in your hair and the sun-
light
reflected in the tide pools of your eyes.
I can't be sure, but I think

You smiled at me before you slid
Beneath the waves again. . . .

Jill continued reading silently down the
page. Then she looked up at Robert with a smile.
"I think I'm beginning to understand a few things
now," she said. "I get the feeling that Cassandra's
interest in marine biology is not just limited to
starfish!"

"I read your poems," Jill said casually as
Cassandra sat brushing out her long black hair in
front of the mirror.

"Did you like them?" Cassandra asked shyly.

"The one about the starfish was good," Jill
said, trying not to smile as she saw Cassandra's
reflection. "But it was like a lot of stuff you've
already written. 'Merman,' however, was very
different."

Cassandra went on brushing. "So are you
practicing to be a mermaid, brushing out your
hair like that?" Jill asked at last.

"I brush my hair every night like this,"
Cassandra said.

"In the hope of luring a merman to your
side?" Jill asked, her eyes holding Cassandra's in
the mirror. "Oh, come on, Cassie," she said at
last. "It's perfectly obvious to me—"

"What is?"

"That it wasn't just dabbling in the tide pools that made your vacation special. What's his name? I want to hear all about him."

Cassandra, who was perpetually cool, actually blushed. "He's wonderful, Jill," she said. "I've never felt this way about a boy before in my whole life. You know me, calm Cassandra who only gets worked up about baby seals and redwood trees. But I took one look at him and, wow!"

"So what's his name? Does he go to school here?"

Cassandra studied her hands. "I think his name is Greg, but I don't know his last name. The Marine Wildlife Center is used by all colleges within a couple hundred mile radius on weekends and over vacations, so he could go to school *anywhere*. I know he doesn't go to Rosemont though. All I do know is that he'll be a teaching assistant part of the semester and that he's incredibly masculine, terribly sensitive, and unspeakably cute."

"So why didn't you ask him his name, or at least tell him who you were," Jill insisted. "Do you think he likes you, too?"

Cassandra played with the ends of her hair. "I've never exactly spoken to him," she said. "I wanted to, Jill. But every time I got near him, my tongue froze."

Jill smiled. "I know the feeling," she said. "So he doesn't even know you exist yet?"

"In a way he does." Cassandra sighed. "He was leading my group one evening, and I slipped on this seaweedy rock. I would have fallen into a deep pool, but he grabbed my arm, and he said, 'Are you okay?' in this deep voice. All I could do was nod like an idiot."

"So that's why you were so insistent that I sign up for marine biology with you," Jill said, grinning. "You don't want me to learn to love the mysteries of the ocean; you want me to teach you the mysteries of love on Saturdays at the center!"

"That's not fair," Cassandra said. "I really am enthusiastic about the marine center, and I do want you to meet the adorable dolphins and seals—but I need help with the boy, Jill. I've just got to meet him, and I don't know how to go about it. I come from a disadvantaged background, remember, going to a girls' boarding school."

Jill shifted uneasily. "Well, I don't know if I can be any help, Cassie," she said. "I haven't made it a habit to go around picking up boys."

"But you haven't done too badly," Cassie said. "Jake is not exactly the worst-looking and least popular guy in the school."

Jill looked horrified. "But I didn't set out to catch him, Cassie. It just sort of happened. It all started when we were sick in the infirmary together, when we sent those anonymous notes back and forth to pass the time, if you remember. I didn't even know who I was writing to. Now that I think about it, I got all my boyfriends as a result of accidents." She had to laugh as she thought of meeting Craig in the fast-foot restaurant, and nearly dropping her purse on Carlo from the Eiffel Tower. "I'm not sure that it ever works when people set out to get a particular guy! Why don't you just go up to him and introduce yourself? After all, you two must have a lot in common. You could make some comment about seals or dolphins, and things could take off from there."

Cassandra threw out both her arms in a gesture of despair. "But don't you see, Jill, when I look at him, every rational thought goes straight out of my head. He'd probably think I was a complete dodo, stuttering and mumbling at him. There's got to be some clever way of meeting him so that he notices me, before I have to speak. Toni could come up with something. Could you call her and ask for her advice? Please, Jill? Please?"

"I can tell it means a lot to you, Cassie," Jill began hesitantly.

"More than anything," Cassie said desperately. "I swear, Jill, if I had to save this boy or a dozen baby whales, I'd dive in and save him."

Jill started to laugh. "So would I, Cassie; he wouldn't weigh so much." She took a look at

46

Cassandra's solemn face. "I'm sorry," she said. "I know I shouldn't make fun, because it's deadly serious to you. Okay, I'll call Toni for you, although I can't predict what crazy scheme she'll come up with. Don't be surprised if she suggests you fake a drowning or leap off a cliff!"

"I'll do anything, Jill," Cassandra said. "But I'm going to need your help to give me courage when we go out to the marine station."

"Don't worry, Cassie, I'll be there," Jill said. "You've been a good friend to me. Besides, now I've registered for the class."

"Would you call Toni now?" Cassandra begged. "I want to give her lots of time to come up with the best plan."

Jill got up. "Oh, okay," she said. "Although I don't know why I'm doing this. I never meddle in other people's affairs. I think I need my head examined. All right, I'm going, I'm going!" And she hurried from the room, leaving Cassandra to stare hopefully at the door.

FIVE

"Toni?"

"Is that you, Jill? Is something wrong?"

"No, everything's fine, why?"

"Because you've only been gone a couple days. I wasn't expecting to hear from you this soon."

"And I wasn't expecting to call you this soon. What took you so long to get to the phone, by the way?"

"It was the first day of dance class."

"Does that have something to do with not wanting to come to the phone?"

"I may never walk normally again, that's all. I had to hobble over here."

"Bad as that, was it?"

"Worse! Jill, legs were never intended to be

stretched into those positions. We all started off at the barre and the instructor said, 'Let's just limber up a bit.' Everyone else lifted up their legs and put their heels on the barre. But that barre is not exactly ankle height, Jill, and I am not a tall person, as you know. It took two hands to lift my heel that high, then I was terrified I'd never get it down again and I'd have to stay there until somebody rescued me. But, at least, I'd done it. Then, Jill, the instructor said, 'Heads onto knees,' and everybody put their noses on their knees. Agony, pure agony. I had no idea how out of shape I was."

"But, it must have been just as bad for the other students, first class of the semester?"

"The other students all stepped straight out of the Bolshoi Ballet. They all look as if they've taken dance since they were three. You remember the sum total of my experience—Miss Marvel and tap class."

"Exaggerating as usual, Toni Redmond. Of course you feel stiff after your first class, but you're a good dancer. You'll catch up quickly even if they've all had more training than you. Remember that great number you did in the spring musical last year?"

"That was just kid stuff, Jill. But I hope you're right about catching up, because I don't know what I'll do if I flunk my theater courses."

"Don't worry, Toni. I panicked after my first

English class, and I ended up loving it and doing well, too. You can't expect to be a champion dancer in a day, although I know you always want instant success. I bet the next time you talk to me, you'll tell me that the teacher has said you're one of the best in the class."

"Fat chance. My legs probably will be permanently wrapped around my neck by the next time you talk to me. But I don't want to waste all your money talking about my latest troubles! What's up?"

"You know I've always got time and money to listen to your troubles, you dope. But what I actually called about was Cassie."

"Cassie?"

"Yes, she wanted me to talk to you right away."

"Why didn't she call me herself then? She knows me well enough to speak to me on the phone."

"She was kind of shy."

"Cassandra? Shy? Are we speaking about the same person who stands in front of bulldozers to stop the destruction of redwood trees? She never struck me as shy."

"She is shy about this one particular subject, which is boys, or rather, a boy. Cassie has fallen in love in a big way, Toni."

"Cassie's in love with something other than a

50

redwood tree or water mammal? Wow, that's a new one."

"Listen, Toni. She asked for your help. She's seen this boy at a marine biology research station on the coast, and she hasn't got the nerve to speak to him. We're going to go up there on a few Saturdays with our marine biology class, and we need to come up with a way to make him notice her."

"You want us to get Cassandra together with a strange boy?"

"That's right. It's got to be some really clever scheme, so he'll notice her without her having to go up and talk to him. Just the sort of thing you're good at."

"Is this the same girl who frequently insists that people should never interfere in other people's love lives?"

"This is different, Toni. The girl is eighteen years old and has never had a real boyfriend. She needs a scheme, and you are an expert at schemes."

"I've never done anything as crazy as stepping off a bridge onto a boy's head, like you did in Venice."

"That was an accident."

"Oh, sure. The fact that it was the right boy, out of the whole of Venice, has always seemed slightly suspicious to me."

"Toni, you know I do not do things like step off bridges on purpose. Stop teasing and start thinking of some brilliant foolproof way to get two people together on the shore, without getting Cassie swept off a rock by a giant wave."

Toni hesitated. "I'll have to think about it, Jill. My mind is blank right now. My brain is busy reacting to the pain in every part of my body. It doesn't have time for thinking. Let me go soak in a nice, hot tub and see what I can come up with—although I get a feeling that maybe we should leave Cassandra to sort this one out by herself."

"I've never known you to chicken out on a challenge, Toni."

"I am not chickening out. It's just that we might be doing Cassandra more harm than good. I mean, look how pleased you were when I fixed you up with a gorgeous date last Thanksgiving vacation!"

"Toni, he was repulsive. He did nothing but talk about himself all evening and grab at me under the table. Cassandra wants to meet this boy desperately, and I just don't have your crazy, warped mind when it comes to weird plots."

"Well, I can't promise anything, but I will put my crazy, warped mind to work, Jill."

"Thanks a million, Toni. I know you'll come up with something. You always do. So how are things, apart from the crazy dance class? Have you started your drama classes yet?"

"I start acting class tomorrow, so I don't know about that yet, but the instructor seems very nice. She's a tall black woman who moves beautifully. I wish she were teaching my dance class, instead of this little man who thumps the floor with a stick."

"And Brandt? Is all going well?"

"Everything is fantastic, beautiful, wonderful, great, and magnificent. Does that give you a hint?"

"I get the feeling you must like this guy! It's nice to have you being the one head over heels in love for a change."

"You mean you're not head over heels in love with Jake?"

"I could be head over heels, but I'm being deliberately cautious. I can remember all the pain of breaking up with Craig and the horrible empty feeling when he was gone. I don't want to get too involved with Jake, I guess, because I know what sort of person he is. He gets tired of things easily. I'm scared he might get tired of me one day soon, and I'm not ready for another broken heart."

"Well, worries like that just don't cross my mind at the moment. I've got Brandt, and he's right here, and he says that he loves me. That's good enough for me now."

"I'm happy for you, Toni, but I have to go now, or I'll have to give up pizza for an entire

53

semester. Will you call me when you think of a foolproof plan for Cassie?"

"Sure, Jill. Take care. Tell Cassie to go for it, if she wants this guy."

"I will. Bye, Toni."

"Bye, Jill."

SIX

January 18

First day of dance class today. What a shock! My whole body feels as if it's been crushed under an eighteen-wheeler. Nobody else seemed to find the exercises hard.

On the way to class I had this daydream about the instructor calling, "Little fair girl at the back, you come up front and show us how it should be done." Of course, I hadn't seen the instructor then. He's this prissy little man, not so tall as I am, and he carries a big stick. He did call out to me in front of the whole class, but not in the way I'd dreamed. Instead, it was, "Little fair girl at the back, no bent knees, that's cheating!" How embarrassing. Now I'm terrified he'll come up to me and tell me I should go back to beginning movement class. Maybe I'll have to start practicing four hours every evening, after I get home from work. But then Mr. Paolini will complain about the thumps on the floor. Maybe Brandt and I could find a place together soon. We've sort of talked about it, but I'm not sure what Mom and Dad would think. I don't suppose Jill would approve.

Oh, speaking of Jill, she called today—crazy phone call! She wanted me to come up with an idea to get Cassie and some strange boy together. That didn't sound like Jill at all. It sounded more like the sort of thing I would do. She's usually the one who stops me from interfering. The funny thing was that I couldn't come up with any idea at all. My mind was just a total blank. In fact, I couldn't help feeling that the whole thing was a bit dumb. Does this mean Jill and I are reversing roles? Have I become the sensible, calm one while Jill's turned into the crazy? That would be funny, wouldn't it? I think it might have something to do with working and being with Brandt. Things like plots to get two people together seem to belong back in high school.

January 20

I'm thinking about quitting my job. Mrs. Thompson has been on my back lately for no reason. The trouble with being the only paid employee is that you get blamed when anything goes wrong. She even snapped at me for talking to Brandt last night. She didn't actually snap—Mrs. Thompson is always subtle, and she never raises her voice. She said, sugary sweet as usual, "Did you already manage to finish those invoices? I see you have time to sit around and chat." Sit around and chat? I'd only said hi, and Brandt was finding out what time I got off to pick me up. Brandt and Mrs. Thompson were extremely polite to each other. I think things are not going well on the new play.

P.S. Today I got my foot onto the barre without lifting it with both hands. Progress. But everyone else could do chaîné turns except me. I didn't even know what they were. When I tried them, I whipped my head the way Michel—that's his name, dumb, isn't it? I bet it's really plain old Michael—told us. I couldn't see where I was going, and I bumped into a group of girls. Everyone laughed. It wasn't funny.

P.P.S. I think drama will be better than dance. Shana seems like a real pro, and she treats us like pros, too. She talks as if she expects all of us to wind up in the professional theater one day, and she assumes we know all the kid stuff about upstage and downstage. We're going to be studying diction and characterization this semester, and there's going to be a play we all have to work on, both onstage and backstage. But it might be Shakespeare. I don't know if I'm too wild about that idea. I could never understand *Hamlet* in high school English. I didn't even realize Ophelia had died until somebody told me. He really should have written a bit more clearly.

January 24

Today started out so well and ended so badly. In dance class Michel taught us a sequence of steps to do across the floor. It was full of names I didn't even know, and it took me awhile to get the hang of it. I asked him if he could go over it again slowly, and someone behind me gave this big sigh and said, "Oh, come on!"

I guess I overreacted—as usual. I've never been known for my calm temperament, have I? I just boiled up. But I didn't explode. I said icily, "I'm sorry if I'm holding up the class for all you pros. Maybe I'd better get back to kindergym where I belong." Then I stalked out before anyone could say anything. Only one mistake—I left my sweats in the dance room, so I had to go back for them later. Even my pride would not allow me to give up an almost new set of sweats. I thought nobody was in the room when I sneaked in, but, just my luck, Michel was bending down going through some records in the corner. He came over to me and said that we should talk. I said there was no point in talking because I obviously wasn't good enough for the class. He said I shouldn't get depressed because some of the girls had been in this same class for a year and a half. I told him I didn't have time to devote a year and a half of my life to one class, and he laughed. He said that what he meant was that it had taken them a year and a half to become as proficient as they were. He didn't mean it would take me that long. He said he could tell from the way I moved that I'd soon catch up. I said I couldn't ever see myself as being as good as some of those girls. Then he said something fantastic. He said that technique wasn't everything. He said that some of those girls were technically excellent, but it was like watching dancing robots. He told me I had presence, which is something not everyone has. People with presence get watched when they enter a stage, even if they are not the best performers. He said I was lucky enough to have that magic something that would make people want to watch me, and that I had a good chance of success. I flew all the way home. I swear my feet didn't touch the sidewalk once. I kept glancing at myself in store windows to see if my presence was radiating as I walked.

I couldn't wait to tell Brandt. I ran straight to his apartment and babbled out the whole thing without taking a breath. But

Brandt wasn't as thrilled as I expected him to be.

It turns out that he and Mrs. Thompson have had a big fight. Mrs. Thompson wanted to cast the new play with all her friends. Brandt told her he wasn't going to direct a second-rate play for anyone and that he was only going to work with the best actors he could find. Mrs. Thompson reminded him that he answered to the board of directors of the Theater Alliance and that he had better learn to fit in if he wanted to keep his job. He told her there was no way he'd have a two-ton whale playing a young girl, even if she was the world's richest woman. Then he quit.

He doesn't seem too worried about not having a job anymore. He says that it's probably best because community theaters are a dead end and that something better will turn up. I feel really sick about it. I got home about an hour ago, and I was shaking as if I had the flu. There aren't a hundred theaters in Seattle. What if something doesn't turn up?

January 25

Mrs. Thompson already hired a new director. That woman does not waste any time, or else she had him waiting for an excuse to get rid of Brandt. He is more her type of person—a fifty-year-old wimp with lots of money. He's also British, and he said he hoped we'd all get to be really good chums. I nearly puked, and I gave him my famous Queen Victoria stare, which, being British, I think he appreciated. After what they did to Brandt, I have to quit my job as soon as possible. I didn't say a word to anyone all day, and on the way home I bought an evening paper to look for new jobs. I should find one pretty easily. After all, I am now an *experienced* person Friday. Maybe I should wait until the crazy rush just before the new play opens and quit then. That would serve them right for treating Brandt that way.

January 26
    Brandt flew to Los Angeles to talk to his director friend in the movies. I feel scared.

January 27
    Today the world ended.

SEVEN

"I don't know about marine biology, Cassie," Jill said as the two girls walked up to the porch of McGregor together. "You promised me cute, furry things like seals and dolphins."

"Dolphins are not furry," Cassandra interrupted.

"Well, at least they smile at you," Jill said. "Those worms we had to dissect today did not smile."

"What do you mean, *we* had to dissect?" Cassandra asked. "I did the dissecting. You just sat there. And you fell off your stool, too."

"It started to wriggle toward me!" Jill complained.

"It was dead. How could it wriggle?"

"It moved. I swear it did."

"Because I knocked it with the scalpel. You are funny."

"I can't help it," Jill said, walking in through the big door behind Cassandra. "I never did like creepy things. And that worm was particularly revolting."

"It will get better, I promise," Cassandra said. "Starfish and sea urchins are much cuter than worms."

"They'd better be," Jill growled.

"Oh, look, you got a phone call from Toni!" Cassandra yelled, snatching the piece of paper from their door. "She must have come up with her brilliant idea—just in time for our first field trip. This message says to call her right away because it's a matter of life and death. Oh, I'm so excited. Jill, go call her!"

"Cassie— I want to wash the wormy smell off my hands first. Give me a break. I'll call her as soon as I've put my stuff away," Jill said, walking into their room and putting her biology book back on the shelf.

"But she says it's a matter of life and death!" Cassie pleaded.

Jill smiled. "You know very well that everything is a matter of life and death with Toni. That just means she has come up with a good idea and she can't wait to share it. Give me two seconds and then I'll call her. Unless you'd rather call her yourself?"

"I'd be too embarrassed," Cassie confided. "I get tongue-tied just thinking about him."

Jill walked into the bathroom and started running the water. "So I'll do it, but no listening in. It makes me nervous to have someone breathing down my neck."

"Spoilsport," Cassandra said, giving Jill a grin as she flopped down on her bed.

Jill walked to the phone down the hall and dialed.

"Okay. Let's hear it," she said as soon as Toni came to her phone. "Go ahead, dazzle us with your brilliance."

"What?" came a muffled voice at the other end.

"Come on, don't be modest!"

"What are you talking about?" asked a stunned voice.

"The idea to get Cassie and the dream boy together. Isn't that what you called about? I couldn't think what else would be a matter of life and death at the moment."

"Oh," Toni's voice said thickly. "Oh, the idea. No, it wasn't that at all."

"Toni?" Jill asked suspiciously. "Toni, have you been crying?"

"For about six hours, nonstop. I didn't believe anyone could have that many tears in her, but they're still coming."

"Toni, what's wrong?"

"He's gone, Jill. Brandt's gone."

"What do you mean, gone?"

"He left. He's gone to Hollywood without me."

"For good? I mean, forever?"

"I don't know. Forever is a long time to talk about, but right now he's not planning to come back." Toni's voice ended halfway between a hiccup and a sob.

"I see." Jill was unsure how to respond. "I can't believe it, Toni. You two seemed so perfect for each other and so happy."

"I thought so, too."

"So what happened? Did you have a fight?"

"No fight. He just left without me. He walked out of his job, Jill, and now he's gone to try to get work in the movies. That friend of his who was making the movie at the ski lodge is trying to help him."

"But that doesn't sound too terrible, Toni. Soon he might be a famous movie director. Just think how that will help you in your career."

"There's only one thing, Jill," Toni said in a small voice. "He doesn't want me around."

"Did he say that?"

A sigh shuddered through the line. "He said his life was in turmoil right now, and he just didn't have time to think about another person."

"But you can understand how he feels, can't you, Toni? You wouldn't have time to think about

Brandt if you went down to audition in Hollywood. That doesn't mean it's all over between you—just put on hold until Brandt can give you the attention you deserve."

"No, it's more than that, Jill. He couldn't even come and say it to me in person. He called from L.A. this morning. He said he still cared about me, but he couldn't ask me to wait around for him, because it might take him years to find out what he wanted out of life. Oh, Jill, what am I going to do? I can't live without him."

"Don't cry, Toni. I really don't believe it's as hopeless as you think. I bet he'll begin to miss you really soon, and one day he'll just turn up on your doorstep."

"I wish I could believe you, Jill, but I don't think so. I know in my heart that I won't ever see him again, and I just don't know how to face that. Remember when we talked about being head-over-heels in love? This is the first time in my life that I've cared that way about anyone. I can actually feel my heart breaking. I just don't know what to do, Jill."

"Why don't you go home to your parents for a while, Toni? You need someone to hug you and take care of you. I wish I could do it myself, but I have my first biology field trip this Saturday, and I can't cut out."

"I don't want my folks to see me like this, Jill. My dad will want to be all the more protective, and my mother will shovel her terrible chicken soup down my throat, and they'll both tell me how I'll get over it and meet someone much nicer. And I couldn't bear that right now."

"I know how it's hurting, Toni, believe me. For a while you think you'll never get over it. But everyone does in the end. At least you've got your dance and acting classes now. Make some new friends. Not boyfriends, but just friends—a group to hang out with, who will care about you. Then if Brandt does come back, it will be wonderful. And if he doesn't, you'll still have a place you belong."

"I just can't think about new friends at the moment. I can't think about anything. My mind is just numb. All I really want to do is fall asleep and not wake up."

"Toni Redmond, don't let me hear you talking like that! You are a terrific person. You are the strongest person I know. You've come through things just as bad as this, like your dad's heart attack. You had to rearrange your whole life then, but you did it. You can come through this, too, if you think about the future. You have a great career ahead of you. You're going to be a famous actress and dancer. And if Brandt doesn't come back to you, at least you'll have the satisfaction of seeing the misery in his face when you become the queen of Hollywood."

Toni managed a ghost of a laugh. "You are

funny," she said. "Somehow I can't even manage to see myself as the queen of Hollywood anymore."

"Then just take one day at a time, Toni. That might be all you can do, right now. Just say to yourself, 'I'm going to make it through Saturday.' Then you can say, 'Well, Saturday was okay. Now I'm going to try Sunday.' Just give yourself little goals like getting praise from your instructor in dance class or buying yourself new makeup. You can do it, Toni. I know you can. I'll be up to see you as soon as I can, I promise. And when I arrive, I want to hear that you've made new friends and learned new things. That's an order, okay?"

"Okay, Jill. I'll try, I suppose. I've got to start by getting a new job. I quit my old one. I couldn't work at the theater anymore. I'd see Brandt's ghost everywhere."

"There you are," Jill said brightly. "Getting a new job can be step one in the Save Toni Redmond Campaign. We'll get Cassandra in on the act. She's an expert on endangered species, and you sound like you're endangered right now."

"Please tell her I'm sorry I didn't come up with her idea," Toni said in a small voice.

"She'll understand. She thinks a lot of you, you know. You have a lot of people who care about you, Toni. You just call anytime you feel like talking."

"Thanks, Jill. I think I'm feeling a little better already. I haven't eaten a thing all day. Maybe I'll try some crackers or something."

"Crackers, my foot. You go to that ice cream place down the street and have one of their giant sundaes. That will put energy back into you."

"Maybe that's not a bad idea. Not a giant one. I couldn't face that—but a small hot fudge, with nuts."

"That's my girl. I'll call you tomorrow, just to see how things are going."

"Thanks, Jill. I'm glad I've still got you around."

"I'll always be around, Toni. You're stuck with me until we collect Social Security together."

"I'll give you a ride to the Social Security office in my gold Cadillac!"

"I can believe it, Toni. Take care of yourself, please."

"I will. Bye, Jill."

"Bye, Toni."

EIGHT

February 4

Today I felt the first glimmer of hope. I haven't even written anything in this diary since—I haven't even wanted to think. I've shut out all my thoughts with loud music and every game show on TV. I still don't want to think about the future or, more especially, the past, but at least I can tell I'm back as part of the world now. I met some wonderful people today. Actually, I didn't exactly meet them—I knocked a wall onto them! This isn't really as bad as it sounds, because it was a theater flat, just painted to look like a wall, but it was still pretty dramatic. I don't think I'll ever get the hang of scenery. If I see something that looks solid, like a pillar or a rock, I expect it to be solid. Anyway, we were taken on a tour of the community college theater for our acting class today, and a group of kids was walking by. I stood aside to let them pass and leaned against a wall because my legs were tired from dance class. Next thing I knew the wall had toppled over. It was a very tall wall, and this boy's head went right through it. He looked very dramatic, standing there with his head sticking out of a wall, while several of his friends were stuck underneath. I thought there was going to be trouble as usual, but you know what they did? They all started laughing, then everyone else started laughing, and my acting teacher said that accidents will happen. I didn't think it the right moment to mention that they seem to happen to me more than other people!

When they had got this guy's head clear of the wall they said they could see how upset I was by the whole thing, and they insisted I come and have some hot chocolate to drink with them after class. They were all into theater, and they were all very concerned about me, so I just started talking. I felt as if I hadn't spoken to anybody in years. I had cut myself off from the rest of the world since Brandt left. I know I have been avoiding calling my folks or talking to Dan or Chris across the hall. I was scared I'd start crying again if I had to explain what I'd been through. But these kids are different. I could have a completely fresh start with them, and

I felt I could really talk to them. When I told them that I had quit my job and was finding it hard to pay my rent, they didn't ask a lot of questions. They just invited me to come and see the big old house they share. They said it was nothing fancy, but if I wanted to crash there for a while I was very welcome. They are really different and interesting and they made me feel like a human being again. I'm going to the house for dinner tonight! Kerry thinks she might be able to get me a job.

"Are you sure you don't want me to go with you?" Cassandra asked Jill as they shivered together in the damp cold of the windswept headland. Below them the bleak huts of the research station huddled in a little valley, just out of reach of the angry waves that crashed onto the shore. It had not stopped raining all that Saturday, and even Cassandra had not managed to spend much time in the tide pools.

"Thanks for offering, but I'd rather go alone," Jill said. "I don't think Toni will want too many people around, and she'd be really embarrassed if she cried in front of you. She hates people seeing her cry, even me."

"It was good that we met those people from the University of Washington, wasn't it?" Cassandra asked. "Now you can get a free ride to Seattle, and you'll only have to pay the bus fare back to Rosemont."

"That's bad enough," Jill said. "But I really have to go. I feel so bad that I couldn't go home earlier, when Toni really could have used a friend, but there hasn't been one day I could skip classes."

"I'm sure she understands," Cassandra said. "And, anyway, it sounds as if she's making progress on her own."

"Yes, she said she'd followed my advice and found some new friends who were helping her a lot. I'm so glad. She's an independent person, but it's not easy being alone in a big city, and she didn't have anyone around who was close to her except Brandt and her parents. I can't wait to meet her new friends."

"And I can't wait to get back to the dorm and into a hot shower," Cassie said, pulling the hood of her poncho down farther over her eyes. "Even dedicated marine biologists do not enjoy sloshing through tide pools in weather like this. Every inch of me is wet and cold."

"And disappointed," Jill said. "Poor Cassie. Three Saturdays here in a row and your dream man hasn't even shown up. I'm beginning to think he only exists in your imagination!"

"He does not," Cassie said sharply. "We've just been coming on different days, that's all. Our paths are not destined to cross yet. Maybe they are not destined to cross until you and Toni come up with a plan. If she seems more cheerful today, Jill, do you think you could ask her about it?"

"I'll see how she is, Cassie," Jill said. "Of course, it would be much easier to find out when he was going to be here if you knew his name. It's a shame Toni wasn't around when you met him."

"Well, she wasn't," Cassandra snapped. "And now I don't know if I'll ever see him again. Nobody else seemed to know who I was talking about."

Jill smiled. "All we found out was that there were around twenty tall, good-looking, dark-haired teaching assistants from different colleges who occasionally come here."

Cassie sighed. "Maybe I'll see him when we're here for the whole week. He'll have to come up for at least one day then, won't he?"

"I hope so, Cassie," Jill said. She glanced up the trail to the parking lot. "You better go. They're loading up the bus."

"See you, Jill. Give my love to Toni and tell her to hang in there. Tell her that's what I'm trying to do right now—just keep on hoping!"

Jill watched Cassandra walk away, a small, fragile figure, buffeted by the fierce wind. Then she turned and went to find the driver of the car to Seattle.

A couple of hours later she was standing alone

in the dark in the city center, feeling like a newly arrived hillbilly as the traffic sped past her and people bumped against her in their rush to cross the street. Jill had always loved the feel of the city—the city-dressed people, the bustle, the bright storefronts, and the slight fishy smell drifting across from the wharves. But the noise and the bustle seemed overpowering after the tranquility of Rosemont and the desolation of the seashore.

She heaved a sigh of relief as she turned into Toni's quiet side street and left the noise and traffic behind her. The apartment house was still as seedy looking. But the little building managed to look friendly, too, as if a person would be welcome there. Jill imagined how surprised and pleased Toni would be to see her. She raced up the front steps and burst in through the open front door.

The house was completely quiet. No strange old woman opened a door on the ground floor to call for her pet dog, Peekaboo. No music blared from behind the two fishermen's door. Jill stood in the dark hallway on the third floor and knocked on Toni's door. There was no answer. Jill knocked again, then turned away in disappointment. She had imagined that Toni would be curled up alone in her room, in need of comfort. She had not considered that Toni would be out early on Saturday evening. *Maybe she's gone to her folks for the weekend,* Jill reasoned. *Or maybe she's just gone out to get a bite to eat, and she'll be home any second.* Jill sat down on the top step, wondering whether to wait or to phone Toni's parents.

She was still sitting there when a head poked up suspiciously from the floor below.

"I thought-a I heard someone going up and not coming down," growled a deep, faintly accented voice. "What you doing up here, little lady? You have come about the apartment?"

"Mr. Paolini?" Jill asked—hesitantly, because the old man with the enormous head of white hair still scared her a little. "I'm Toni's friend, Jill. I've been to visit a couple of times before. I was waiting for Toni to get back. You don't happen to know where she's gone, do you?"

Mr. Paolini went on staring at her. "You-a going to have to wait a long time then," he said dryly. "Because she don't-a live here no more."

"What?" Jill stammered. "Toni Redmond? She moved out?"

"That's-a right. You just missed her. She moved out a couple days ago."

"But why?" Jill demanded. "Where did she go?"

Mr. Paolini shrugged his shoulders.

"But didn't she say anything about where she was moving?" Jill asked. "Who came to help her with her stuff?"

"A bunch-a crazy kids, that's who," Mr.

Paolini said. "These crazy kids kept-a running up and down the stairs, disturbing all my tenants. If that's the kind of friends she's-a making now, then good riddance, because my tenants no like crazy people."

"How do you mean crazy, Mr. Paolini?" Jill asked hesitantly.

Mr. Paolini rolled his eyes toward heaven. "You seen the way they dress, these kids?" he began but didn't continue.

Jill tried again. "So she didn't say why she was moving out or if she was going back home?"

Mr. Paolini already had turned to walk back down the stairs. "I tell you, she didn't say nothing. She just comes up to me a few evenings ago and says 'Mr. Paolini, I'm going to be moving out.' That's-a all."

"I'll just call her folks. They'll know her new address."

"Okay, little lady, you do that," Mr. Paolini said. "And tell her I miss her, in spite of her accidents and her thumping on the floor."

As soon as she was outside, Jill hurried down to the nearest pay phone and dialed Toni's parents' house.

"Why, Jill, how nice to hear from you," Toni's mother said excitedly. "Are you up visiting? Are we going to see anything of you?"

"I wondered if Toni was with you right now," Jill said. "I've come up to see her."

"She's not here, honey," Toni's mother said. "I take it you've already been by her apartment. Doesn't that old Italian man know where she is? He's usually so nosy about who goes in and out there."

Jill opened her mouth to speak and then closed it again. It dawned on her that Mrs. Redmond had no idea that Toni had moved.

"Er—how long since you've seen Toni?" Jill asked cautiously.

"Oh, she hasn't been back since the beginning of the semester," Mrs. Redmond said. "You know her—when she has a hectic social life she forgets all about her poor old folks. You could try Brandt's place—she might be over there."

"Yes, thank you," Jill mumbled. "Nice talking to you, Mrs. Redmond." Then she put the phone down. So Toni had not even told her folks about Brandt yet. Thank heavens Jill hadn't given it away! She came out of the phone booth and stood in the darkness, wondering what to do next. Why had Toni told no one where she was going? Could she have decided to do something terrible? Frightening thoughts whirled through Jill's mind.

Stop panicking, Jill told herself severely. *Just think about this logically. She must have moved in with the new friends she told you about. If she were going to do anything desperate, she wouldn't have bothered to move her stuff. She just didn't want to tell her parents* or me until she got settled and found a new job. You know what Toni's like. She's proud; she doesn't want anyone to feel sorry for her.

The thoughts comforted Jill a little. The remaining problem was how to find where Toni had gone. Students who moved probably had to register a change of address with the community college, but there was only the slimmest chance anybody would be in the college offices on a Saturday night. It was worth a try. It was also the only thing Jill could think of doing.

The college campus was not completely deserted as she climbed up an outdoor flight of steps leading to the main buildings. Lights were on in the auditorium building, and people were starting to gather for a show of some kind. Most of them looked more like regular theatergoers than like students. The student center was also open, and clusters of students wandered in and out. Jill stopped a friendly-looking foursome to ask if the administration offices were likely to be open. The group was sure they weren't. "Look, it's Saturday night," a girl said. They walked away, glancing back at Jill as if they suspected she was slightly crazy.

Jill was growing increasingly frustrated, worried, and hungry. She had almost decided to take the bus out to her own parents' house for the night when she heard the tinkling of bells coming across the campus and heading for the auditorium. It was a haunting noise that made Jill think of caravans of camels in the desert, nomadic processions, and exotic dancers. She turned toward it and saw a line of people coming toward her. They were wearing long flowing robes in bright purples, oranges, and yellows. Some of the boys had shaven heads; some of the girls were almost hidden behind long manes of black hair. As they got nearer, Jill could hear the chanting, although she couldn't understand the words. Many of them carried buckets on which the words "Purple People" were painted in big letters. These buckets they waved in the faces of everyone they passed. Most people laughed nervously and dropped coins into the buckets. Others found their tickets in a hurry and made for the theater door.

The young beggars were very insistent. "Come on, give to the Purple People," several of them insisted as they approached students who had emerged from the student center.

"Oh, come on, guys," one person they cornered said nervously, "I've already supported you. I've got to eat, too."

"Yeah, but you get food to eat every day," a tall boy in purple growled. "How about thinking of people who don't get meals every day?"

The boy dipped into his pocket and coins clattered into the bucket. The group moved on, coming steadily toward Jill. Jill had read about strange cults, but she hadn't actually seen any of them before. She watched in fascinated horror as they came nearer. She put her hand nervously into her pocket, fumbling for any loose change in case they pressured her.

"Money for the Purple People," a voice called out, loud and clear. Jill whipped around as if she had been shot. The group had almost passed, but at the back was a small, blond figure dressed in a long, shapeless, purple garment.

"Toni?" Jill shouted in horror. "Toni, is that you?"

The small, blond figure left the group and came across to Jill. In addition to the purple robe, she was wearing beads with a bell on them around her neck and a beaded headband just above her eyebrows.

"Jill," she screamed. "What are you doing here?"

"I was just about to ask you the same question, Toni," Jill said uneasily.

Toni smiled. "That's simple. I'm collecting donations right now."

"But who are these people?" Jill demanded. "What are you doing dressed like this?"

"These are the new friends I told you about," Toni explained, recoiling from Jill's unexpected attack. "Meet the Purple People."

"Some friends," Jill said, grabbing Toni's arm and trying to drag her to a more private place.

"Toni, how could you do such a dumb thing?" she hissed.

"What do you mean?" Toni asked angrily. "And will you let go of my arm. You're embarrassing me."

"I mean, getting yourself mixed up with people like this. You know what these people are like, Toni!"

"Yes, I do know," Toni said calmly. "And I think they are terrific. I fit in perfectly from the moment I met them."

Jill stared at her in horror. "You feel that you fit in—walking around chanting and begging?" she asked, just controlling herself.

Toni shook herself free of Jill. "Let me explain," she said. "We are not begging. We are simply raising money for—"

"I don't want to hear about it," Jill said. "I've read enough to know how people like this get new recruits."

"What are you talking about?" Toni asked. "Have you gone completely out of your mind? These are just perfectly normal, ordinary fun people."

"Oh, sure," Jill said bitterly. "I could tell that instantly. Mainly by the bells around the feet and the shaven heads." She stepped toward Toni again. "Look, Toni, come with me now, before it's too late."

Toni shrank back as if Jill were a slightly

suspicious stranger. "Of course I'm not coming with you. What's the matter with you, Jill?"

"Toni, come on, we're going to be late," a deep voice called from the line.

Toni looked up, torn between leaving the argument unfinished and going to join her friends. "Look, Jill, I can't stay now," she said. "But I think you've got the wrong impression about things. Why don't you come with us? Then you can see what we're really like and maybe come back to spend the night at our house. Did I tell you I moved in with them? It's a little primitive, but otherwise great."

"I can imagine," Jill said dryly. "Look, Toni, I can't hang around, and I don't want to meet these people. I'd only get angry."

"I never thought that you were such a prejudiced person," Toni snapped. "Just because people look a little different from you, you decide they are not worth meeting. You jump to conclusions, and then you don't let me—"

"I don't want to hear, Toni," Jill yelled. "I want you to come with me, right now. We'll go back to your folks' for the night and talk things over."

"I've told you before I can't come with you now," Toni shouted. "What's gotten into you, Jill?"

The tall boy in purple walked back to Toni and took her hand. "Come on," he said. "You can talk to your friend later, but now we've got an important job to do."

Toni looked at Jill and shook her head. "I'm sorry that you feel this way, Jill," Toni said icily. "Because I don't want you for a friend if you can't accept my new friends and let me choose my own life."

"If that's the way you want it," Jill said shakily, "then fine with me. Choose them instead of me. But I want you to know that I'll always be available if you need help, Toni. One day you'll come to your senses and realize you've made a mistake, and I hope you're not afraid then to call me."

Then she turned and ran off down the steps, before Toni could see her cry.

"What was that all about?" the boy asked Toni. Toni shrugged her shoulders in embarrassment. "I don't know what's gotten into her," she said. "I tried to tell her what we're doing, but she wouldn't even listen. She wouldn't even stay to meet anyone. It's not like her at all. I think she may be hurt that I'm not running to her for all the answers anymore."

The boy shrugged. "People change," he said. "Come on, we've hardly got time to get our makeup on." Toni turned and followed him through the back door of the auditorium. A poster taped to the door proclaimed: "The Purple People. A New And Zany Review. Come And Laugh With Our Own Crazy Comedy Company. Proceeds To World Famine Relief."

NINE

"So what can I do about Toni?" Jill asked Jake the next day. She had caught the last bus and arrived back at Rosemont, exhausted both physically and emotionally, at one in the morning. She had crept into her room so that she didn't wake Cassandra, then fallen into a sleep of troubled dreams. Men in purple robes turned into piles of grape gelatin and threatened to suffocate Toni, who was lying in a huge rice bowl. Jill couldn't pull Toni out of the bowl. Toni said she was warm and comfortable, and she didn't seem to notice that the gelatin was rising around her and would finally flow over her.

In the morning she told Cassie all about her encounter with Toni, but Cassie didn't give her the reaction she had wanted. She said that everyone should be free to go her own way and that it sounded as if Toni had found contentment. Jill, her nerves still frazzled, had snapped at her. Cassandra, who hated any sort of fight, simply walked out, leaving Jill alone to feel terrible.

After a breakfast of hot chocolate and a bite of a piece of french toast, Jill had gone to Jake's room. Jake, who did not rise early on Sunday mornings, listened with half-opened eyes while Jill sat on the edge of his bed and poured out the whole story. "And now I don't know what to do next," she moaned.

Jake finally managed to open his eyes fully and look at her. "Just my luck," he complained, "the one time she comes to sit willingly on my bed, all she wants to do is discuss her best friend."

"Be serious, Jake," Jill said. "I'm really worried about her, you know."

Jake reached out and took Jill's hand. "I can see you are," he said kindly. "But there's really nothing you can do. After all, it's her life, and she's an adult. I can't see Toni belonging to this group for too long." A smile crossed his lips.

"But it's true, Jake," Jill insisted. "If only you could have seen them in their robes, chanting and begging. It was horrible. I know Toni normally wouldn't have joined them, but she was really down after Brandt left. That's how cults get their recruits. When a person has nowhere else to turn. Now they'll never let her out again."

Jake sat up and enveloped Jill in his arms. "You've got to stop worrying," he said. "Toni's pretty tough. I think it would take a lot to brainwash her. She's also not stupid. Give her some time, Jill. In a couple of weeks she'll meet a good-looking guy, and suddenly the world will seem bright and rosy again, and she'll be back to her old self."

"I wish I could believe that," Jill said. "But a few weeks may be too late. These cults don't let people just walk out when they feel like it."

"As I said before, it looks like there's nothing that you can do about it, Jill. Maybe all friendships are not meant to last forever. Maybe Toni and you have grown apart."

"But I can't believe it would end like this," Jill said. "I know Toni better than anyone else does. I can't just let her be swallowed up by the Purple People without a fight."

"But you have to give her time," Jake said patiently. "You know Toni better than I do, and even I know that Toni could never be forced to do something she didn't want to do. You can't make her leave if she doesn't want to, Jill. Wait until living with a group like that has started to annoy her. Then you might not have to do much persuading."

"But she said she doesn't want to see me again." Jill could hear her voice quivering.

"I'm sure she'll change her mind about that, too," Jake said. "And in the meantime, how about paying some attention to your poor, neglected boyfriend? If you continue to ignore him he may run away with the Purple People, too!"

Jill started to smile. "I can just imagine you living in a cult," she said, shaking her head. "You'd look so sweet in one of those long nightshirts, or maybe with a yellow bedsheet draped around you."

Jake laughed. "It doesn't really sound like me," he said. "Maybe I'd just better find myself a new girlfriend, instead."

Jill tightened her arms around his neck. "Don't do that," she whispered, nestling her cheek against his shoulder.

"Well, I'm not sure," Jake went on. "The girlfriend I've got right now divides all her time between her daffy friend in Seattle and studying sea urchins on the weekends in a windy shack on the coast."

"I do not, Jake Randall," Jill said, tickling his neck. "I've been there precisely three times."

"But what about the week after this?" Jake demanded. "I'm being deserted for the whole of Washington's birthday week because you have to study your sea urchins."

"You could come along if you wanted," Jill said.

"No, thanks. I don't go for windy shacks on seashores, not when I have to share them with a hundred other people. Now if it were you and I, alone together for a week . . ."

"We're alone together right now," Jill whispered. "And all you're doing is talking."

"We can change that," Jake said as he pulled her close to him.

TEN

Jill stared out of the window as the gray countryside flashed past. At the back of the bus some boys had begun to sing, "Ninety-nine bottles of beer on the wall." They were already down to sixty-four, but Jill hardly noticed the noise anymore. She was recalling all the things she had done with Toni. She saw the seven-year-old with two missing front teeth and swimming-pool-green hair choosing to sit next to her in the second grade. She saw the two of them lying in their sleeping bags watching late-night horror movies on TV. Toni was an indistinguishable bump most of the time because she was too scared to look, Jill was rooted to the screen, terrified. The next day Toni would act very cool about the movie. "We saw this great movie last night," she would boast. "It was on at two A.M. We snuck downstairs to watch it. It wasn't scary at all."

"Are you still brooding about Toni, Jill?" Cassandra asked from the next seat.

"You must be a mind reader," Jill admitted. "However hard I try, I can't put her out of my mind. I keep remembering all the funny little things that happened to us. The time she tried out for the chorus line and nearly pulled the other girls off the stage, the time we were roller-skating car hops and we collided with full trays, the time she thought an old man on a train in Europe was a kidnapped scientist and dragged me with her to alert the conductor."

Cassandra smiled. "It sounds as though you might be safer without her," she said.

"I'd be safer," Jill agreed. "But life wouldn't be so interesting. She stopped my life from becoming boring."

"You have other friends now," Cassandra said. "You have me and Jake. Are you trying to say that we're boring?"

"Of course not," Jill said. "But you met Toni. You know she's different. Wild things happen when she's around—at least, wild things used to happen. . . ." Her voice trailed off as she turned to stare out the window.

"I bet she'll start feeling bad about what happened," Cassandra said. "I'm sure you'll hear from her soon."

"You didn't see how she was," Jill said hopelessly. "She practically ordered me out of her life."

"But you've had big fights before, haven't you?" Cassandra asked. "And you've always made up again."

Jill shook her head. "This was different. All those times we yelled at each other and said dumb things, then we went home, realized what we'd said, and made up again. This sounded so final, and I was the only one yelling. She still had that stupid saintly look on her face." She heaved a big sigh. "I guess it really is the end this time, Cass. For the past week I've been waiting for a phone call. I hoped she'd realize—"

"And you didn't even get a chance to ask her about my boy-catching scheme," Cassandra said lightly.

"I don't think you'd want the kind of suggestion she'd come up with these days," Jill said. "She'd probably have you meditate with him or wave incense in his face."

"The way things are going for me, he won't even show up this week," Cassandra said with a sigh. "I'm beginning to wonder if you were right, maybe he was just somebody I created in my mind. Maybe he is too good to be true. And even if he's there, I can't think of one good reason why he'd notice me."

Jill turned and looked at Cassandra. "Hey,"

she said firmly, "both of us can't be depressed at the same time, you know."

"I know," Cassie said. "But I can't help it, Jill. All my life, I've been the sort of person who didn't need anyone else. When other girls were drooling over football players and rock stars, I was pinning up pictures of baby seals on my wall. But suddenly something has hit me. I'm tired of seeing everyone else walking around in pairs. I want it to happen to me, too."

Jill gave Cassie an encouraging smile. "It will, Cassie. I'll do everything I can to help you, I promise. I've been so caught up with my own worries that I didn't have time to notice you were depressed. Let's both stop worrying and try a little positive thinking."

"Good idea," Cassie said, "only we better start the thinking very soon. My stomach starts tying itself in knots as soon as we get close to the research station, and all logical thoughts fly right out of my head."

"We'll start right now," Jill said with determination. "Plan to Help Cassie Meet Mr. X. Let's think—why don't you make a list of very intelligent questions to ask if he leads your group?"

Cassie shook her head. "I don't want him to think of me as a brain. Besides, I'd probably get too tongue-tied. The questions would come out garbled."

"Okay," Jill said, running her fingers

through her hair as she thought. "You brought your guitar with you. How about offering to play at one of the evening get-togethers? I can just see it—the firelight reflecting on the guitar and your face, your hair cascading down as you sing a haunting love song—"

"And me forgetting the words because I notice he's in the room?" Cassie finished for her. "It's no use, Jill. I know I can't trust myself to behave normally when he's around. Whatever plan we come up with, I've got to play a passive part in it—like a prop in a stage play."

"Do you think he'll notice a prop?" Jill asked.

"Maybe we weren't so wrong when we thought about dangerous things," Cassie said thoughtfully. "Maybe if he had to rescue me. Perhaps I'd look appealing, lying half-drowned in his arms."

"Cassie!" Jill said, horrified. "You're prepared to drown to meet him? Are you that desperate?"

"I wasn't suggesting really drowning, Jill," Cassandra said. "But if we could stage an accident of some sort, right where he is about to appear—"

"And what if he doesn't show up and you die of the cold, or some nerd with mismatched socks dives in after you instead?" Jill asked, laughing.

Cassie smiled. "So it needs careful planning," she said. "And there is an element of risk involved. But I'm thinking about that big rock that juts out right below the cabins. I could wait until he was about to come out of his cabin and then pretend to be trapped on that rock with the tide rising around me—"

Jill thought for a minute. "Possibly," she said, "but how can we know when he'll come out of his cabin and if he'll come out alone or if someone else will get to you first?"

"You'll hide up next to the cabin and spy for me," Cassie said. "When you see him heading out the door, signal me, and I'll pretend to be trapped and start yelling for help. You get his attention by grabbing him and pointing out that there's a girl in danger of drowning."

Jill had to laugh. "It sounds wild, Cassie, but I'm willing to give it a try for you. But I can't promise to hold back all the nerds who want to save you first."

"I'll take the risk," Cassie said. "Anything for a slim chance that he'll notice me."

"I hope it works for you, Cass," Jill said.

A half hour later the bus drew up at the Wildlife Center's bleak collection of huts perched on the rocky seashore. Wisps of fog clung to cliffs in the distance. As the restless group climbed down from the bus, they were met by the barking of sea lions and the strong smell of seaweed washed up on the shore. The cold was biting.

"This is like going into the army," one girl

said, putting on her backpack and looking down toward the row of huts.

"Worse than the army," a boy commented.

"It used to be an army base in World War Two," another boy informed them.

"Only they moved out because it was too cold and painful for them," the girl said.

Cassandra and Jill followed the group down the slope toward the huts. Cassandra almost broke into a run, and Jill could see the excitement on her face.

Poor Cassie, she thought. *I hope this crazy scheme works out for her. I hope he's here this time.*

According to the schedule passed out on the bus, everyone had a half hour to find a bunk and explore the area before orientation. While Jill arranged her gear, Cassandra went to find the bathrooms. She came flying back into the room a few moments later. "I've seen him. He's here!" she whispered excitedly. "I just glanced out through the bathroom window, and I saw him going into the last cabin in that row. Are you ready? Can we put the plan into action right now?"

"Right now?" Jill echoed. "I don't know, Cassie. Shouldn't we wait to see if we need it? Maybe you'll have a perfectly easy chance to get to know him without all this drama."

Cassie shook her head. "No, I'm not going to

let him get away this time, Jill. Let's do it right now. We've got him trapped in the cabin, and I know I'll lose my nerve if I keep waiting and thinking about it."

Jill pulled on her parka. "All right," she said with a sigh. "It's crazy, but I guess I promised. Let's go."

Cassie dragged Jill down to the beach. "See that cabin. That's the one," she said, pointing to a small log structure that couldn't have contained more than four people. "Go peek in the window and see if anyone else is in there."

"I can't just go look in somebody's window, Cass. What if he's changing?"

"Just a quick peek?" Cassie pleaded.

"You're worse than Toni," Jill said. "I thought I did the craziest things for her, but this is worse than any of them."

Jill climbed up to the cabin and walked past the side of it, as if she were in a hurry to get somewhere else.

"You're in luck," she told Cassie as she returned in a loop to the rocks. "There seems to be only one person in there. I didn't stop to look carefully, but I saw just one guy bending down to get something out of a suitcase."

"I'm in luck," Cassie sang out. "This is my lucky day, Jill. I can feel it. Now I'm going to climb down on this rock and pretend my foot is caught in a crevice, okay? As soon as you see him coming out his front door, you run up to him and say, 'Come quick! There's a girl trapped down on that big rock.' I'll yell for help as if I'm in great pain."

"I'll feel like a fool," Jill muttered.

"Then please feel like a fool for me," Cassie begged.

"Okay, Cass," Jill said with a smile. "Good luck. I hope it works, so we don't have to go through any more scenes like this."

Cassie turned and began to pick her way over the first rocks out to a big flat one. Waves were already licking at the edge of it, and it was richly covered with seaweed from spending most of its life under the water.

Jill watched as Cassie found a good position, where a deep crack almost divided the rock in two, and forced her foot into the crevice. Then Jill stood alert, directly in line with the front door.

Minutes passed. Nobody came or went. Jill glanced at her watch and saw that only fifteen minutes remained until the orientation began. Cassie looked up at Jill. Jill shook her head. More minutes passed. Jill wondered if the boy could be taking a nap. She began to feel very cold. She thought that Cassie must have been feeling even colder, half sitting on wet weed. The tide was beginning to come in, and waves were starting to lap higher on the rock.

Without warning, Jill heard the front door open. She leaped into action.

"Come quickly," she yelled, rushing toward the tall, dark boy who was blinking in the bright light as he emerged from the cabin. "There's a girl down on that rock. I think she's trapped there. . . ." Her voice trailed away to nothing as she looked at the boy closely for the first time. At the same moment, his eyes focused on her. "Jill?" he said, at the same moment that she cried, "Craig!"

ELEVEN

Jill's ex-boyfriend continued to stare at her. "Jill?" he asked again, surprise and amusement playing on his face. "What on earth are you doing here?"

"Marine biology," Jill stammered. "I had to do a science this semester, and I signed up for marine biology."

"How about that?" Craig said, still shaking his head as though she were a vision who might vanish at any second. "I'm working here this year part-time, helping out Professor Jensen, my adviser."

"That's amazing," Jill said. "I remember— you took marine biology last year, didn't you? You must really like it to keep coming back."

"I get more interested in it all the time,"

Craig said. "I'm assisting with some research into the return of the sea otter population."

"Then you ought to meet my roommate," Jill said. "She's crazy about furry things that swim —" She broke off with her mouth open, suddenly remembering Cassie down on the rock.

At that moment came a splash and a scream from the beach. "Oh, my goodness, Cassie!" Jill yelled. "Quick!" She turned to Craig. "My roommate's down there on that big rock."

As they turned to look, a wave broke over the surface of the rock, completely drenching Cassie. Cassie was standing up now, yelling and waving to Jill. "Hurry please!" she was yelling. "I really have got my foot caught."

"Oh, no," Craig muttered, springing ahead of Jill. "Of all the crazy things!" He leaped down the rocks and knelt down to wrestle with Cassie's trapped foot. Another, higher wave crashed around them.

"We'll have to leave your shoe behind," Craig said, fumbling with the laces and pulling her free. He carried her up onto a rock above the tide just as a much larger wave completely submerged the rock she had occupied. Jill reached out to Cassie and helped her—white faced, soaking, and shivering—up onto the safety of the pathway. Craig, almost as wet as Cassie by now, clambered up after her. The threesome walked quickly up the path to the cabins. "Of all the dumb things,"

Craig said, looking at Cassie severely. "Didn't they give you any rules about shoreline safety? You just broke two of the most important. Number one, beware of freak waves. Never stand out on exposed rocks, even if they do seem to be above the water line. Number two, all assignments are to be completed with a buddy."

"I'm sorry," Cassie said, her teeth chattering.

Craig's expression softened a little. "What were you doing out there anyway? Classes haven't even started yet."

"I—er," Cassie began, but Jill interrupted. "She's doing research into starfish, and she wanted to check out some theory of hers the moment we arrived. She's an experienced marine biologist, you know."

Craig came to a halt next to his cabin. He looked from Cassie to Jill and shook his head. "Well, she's not going to be one for very long if she catches pneumonia," he said. "You better get her changed in a hurry. And I think I'd better change myself." He stared down at his sodden jeans and dripping parka.

"I'm sorry I got you all wet," Cassie said in a small voice. "Thank you for rescuing me."

Craig managed to smile. "It's okay," he said. "But just consider yourself lucky that I happened to be in my cabin when you got yourself trapped. It only takes a few minutes for that rock to be completely under water, you know. Take her back and get her a hot drink, Jill."

"Okay, Craig," Jill said and led the shivering, dejected Cassie toward their cabin.

Fortunately the cabin was empty when Jill and Cassie entered. Everyone else had gone to orientation. "I can't believe I made such a mess of things," Cassie said as she dried off after a hot shower. Jill was attempting to dry Cassie's clothes under her hair dryer. "Now he knows who I am, and he thinks I'm the biggest idiot in the world. There's no hope left. I feel like such a fool." She stopped suddenly and looked at Jill with new interest. "He called you Jill," she said. "How come he knew your name?"

Jill smiled. "He knew my name because his name is Craig Wexler. He's the ex-boyfriend about whom you've heard so much."

"That's the famous Craig?" Cassie stammered.

"That's him," Jill said. "I don't know why I didn't put two and two together before this. I knew he'd taken marine biology last year."

"Your boyfriend," Cassie murmured.

"My *ex*-boyfriend," Jill said firmly. "All over and forgotten. You have nothing to worry about from me, Cass. He's all yours if you want him."

Cassie sighed. "The big question is whether he wants me," she said. "I could hardly have made a worse first impression, could I, Jill?"

Jill smiled. "At least he won't forget you in a hurry," she said. "Come on, if we hurry, we can make the end of the orientation session."

Jill might as well have skipped the entire orientation session. Her thoughts kept drifting toward the afternoon's strange twist of events. She wasn't surprised that Craig was the boy Cassie had fallen for. He was cute, and he was charming. But as far as Jill was concerned, her own attraction to him was a thing of the past.

It's good that we're meeting again this way, Jill thought to herself back at the cabin. *This will prove that I can act like a mature adult. He'd be a great boyfriend for Cassie. He might make her a little less weird, and she might make him a little less conventional. I'll get them together at the party tonight!*

She was very proud of herself as she walked with Cassie toward the park ranger's lodge where the welcome party was to be held. The lodge, the only truly civilized building at the center, warmed them with a huge fire roaring in the fireplace. Waves of conversation washed over the girls as they entered the meeting room.

"Looks good, doesn't it?" Jill whispered to her friend "Let's stock up on the hot chocolate and cookies, and then we'll go find Craig. . . ."

Her voice trailed away as a shrill laugh made her look toward the fireplace. Craig stood with his arm resting easily on the thick stone mantelpiece. The firelight played on his face and hair, and he was smiling down at a petite blond girl who was still laughing as she gazed up at him adoringly. Jill felt as if she'd been slapped in the face. She was totally unprepared for the great surge of jealousy that seized her. *Don't be so childish,* she tried to tell herself. *All that was over and finished long ago. It's not as if you've been mooning over Craig for the past few months. You have Jake; you didn't want to be tied to Craig anymore. Did you think he was going to enter a monastery the moment you two broke up?*

Reasoning with herself was useless. Jill couldn't stop her heart from hammering as she watched Craig. She had forgotten how handsome he was. At that moment, the firelight made his eyes sparkle and accentuated the tiny creases that appeared around them as he smiled. Jill remembered when he had smiled like that at her.

Cassie broke Jill's trance by grabbing her arm. "Looks like the seat next to him is already taken," she whispered. "What chance do I possibly have against someone who looks like that?"

Jill pulled herself together with a great effort. "Maybe he's just flirting with the first pretty girl he's met tonight," she said. "I remember he does like to flirt." She turned to Cassie and smiled. "You look very nice tonight," she said. "Why don't we go over and break up the party? Then you can be witty and intelligent, and he'll see how much deeper you are than some giggling blond thing."

Cassie made a face. "Fat chance," she said. "But nice try anyway."

"Come on," Jill said firmly. "We're going over there whether you like it or not." She tossed back her hair and pushed her way through the crowd. Craig stopped suddenly in midsentence when he saw her. Jill couldn't be sure in the dim firelight, but she thought he blushed.

"Oh, hi, Jill," he said hesitantly. "Enjoying the party?"

"We just got here," she said. "But I can see you're having a good time."

Craig smiled uneasily. "Er, let me introduce you," he said, turning to the girl beside him. "Jill, this is Alexandra, who's in my marine biology class at Thomson. Alexandra, this is Jill, who's an old friend from home."

Alexandra turned a pair of big, blue eyes on Jill and twitched her lips into a smile. "Oh, how nice to meet someone who knew Craig when he was a little boy," she said. "You'll have to tell me all the horrible secrets about him. Was he cute when his front teeth were missing?"

"I didn't know him when he was that young," Jill answered as sweetly as she could. "But I remember seeing some pictures of him from grade school, and he always looked serious and well behaved. I don't think he ever did the terrible things little boys are supposed to do."

Alexandra turned to smile up at Craig. "Remind me to ask your mom to see the photo albums when we go to your house," she said.

Again Jill felt real, physical pain. *So much for the first-pretty-girl theory,* she told herself. *This is not someone he's just flirting with.* The stabbing pain grew more intense as Jill thought of another girl being welcomed at Craig's house, sitting at the big oak dining table while Mrs. Wexler spread out the photo albums, leaning over them with Craig's head close to hers.

"So how are you enjoying your marine bio class so far?" Craig asked Jill politely. "Have you been coming down on Saturdays?"

"Yes, we have," Jill answered, also politely. "And it's been freezing or raining every time. I don't think I'm cut out for outdoor education. I only came because Cassandra is so interested in marine biology and kept nagging me until I signed up."

Craig turned toward Cassandra. "So you're a science major, are you? What's your area of concentration?"

"I'm into ecology," Cassandra said hesitantly. "Mainly the preservation of sea mammals. Although I did find the starfish fascinating when I was here over the winter break."

Craig smiled at her politely. "Oh, yes, I

remember you now. You came down here in January and did some volunteer work on the starfish and sea urchins project with Professor Hutchins, didn't you? How did that go?"

"It was very interesting," Cassandra said.

Craig nodded. "You must get together with Alexandra," he said, turning back to the girl who had moved noticeably closer to him. "She's an expert on sea mammals in this area, aren't you?"

"Hardly an expert," Alexandra said. She wrapped her arm through his in a gesture that said clearly, "Keep away, strange girl, this one is mine!"

"She's being too modest," Craig said, smiling down at her fondly. "She's worked here for the past two summers and tagged hundreds of seals."

Jill stared coldly at Alexandra. Her being an accomplished scientist compounded Jill's jealousy. Alexandra looked so little and helpless— and pretty, Jill had to admit. It was hardly fair that she should look helpless and pretty *and* be an expert seal tagger!

"How interesting," she said flatly. "So are you planning to make seals your life's work?"

"I haven't decided yet," Alexandra said. "I'm also interested in chemistry, and I may go into medicine."

Jill stopped herself before she said, how interesting, again.

"And how are things down at Rosemont?" Craig asked Jill.

"Fine. Everything's fine," Jill answered. *Look at us,* she thought. *We are being so polite to each other. As if we were strangers who had just met!*

"Oh, you're at Rosemont!" Alexandra said, showing positive interest in Jill for the first time. "I thought about going there."

Again Jill felt herself forcing a smile. *I can't stand this another second.* She put her hand to her forehead. "If you guys will excuse me," she said, "I've really got the worst headache. I think I had better get to bed and sleep it off."

"I'm sorry about that," Craig said. "Would you like me to walk you back to your cabin?"

"Oh, no, I'll be fine," Jill said, her eyes holding his steadily for a moment before she looked away. "I just need a couple of aspirin and then a good, long sleep. You know I'm a terrible traveler by bus. I always feel sick for hours afterward."

"I remember," Craig said. His eyes smiled at her in recollection for a moment.

"I hope you feel better in the morning," Alexandra chimed in. "We've got some terrific things planned, and there are pups in the sea lion colony."

"I'm sure I'll be fine," Jill said.

"I'll walk back with you," Cassandra said, stepping up to Jill.

"Oh, you don't have to leave because of me, Cassie," Jill said. "Why don't you stay and meet people?"

"No, I'm pretty tired, too," Cassie said. "Near drownings do have that effect. Excuse us, folks." She shepherded Jill toward the door.

The cold night air took Jill's breath away. She turned to smile at her friend. "You didn't have to come, Cassie," she said.

"Are you joking?" Cassie asked. "Do you think I wanted to stand there while Miss Perfect told us how she managed to win a Rhodes Scholarship in the same year she won Miss World?"

Jill laughed. "She was totally sickening, wasn't she?"

Cassie nodded. "It's a good thing you're totally over Craig, or someone like that might make you want to kill," she said, laughing.

"Yes," Jill said as she pushed open the cabin door ahead of her friend. "It's a good thing."

TWELVE

In spite of her fatigue and the two aspirin, Jill lay awake a long time. Then her sleep was full of confused dreams, as she tossed on the uncomfortable cot. When she woke in the morning, she was no less confused. *What's the matter with me?* she wondered. *I don't really want Craig back, do I?* She switched her thoughts back to Jake, back to Rosemont. She remembered laughing as Jake walked her to the bus, his arm around her shoulder, describing to her the horrors she would encounter at camp that week. He had told her about people who had had legs bitten off by great white sharks, who were stung to death by killer jellyfish, or who had been eaten, boat and all, by enormous blue whales. He had told it so funnily that Jill had ached with laughter. And he hadn't foreseen that the greatest danger would come from meeting someone she hadn't expected to see again.

I really do miss Jake, she told herself firmly. *And I'm only feeling like this about Craig because he has another girl with him. I'm just being childish. Every time I think I've grown up, something happens to show me that I still have a long way to go. But today I'm going to behave like an adult around Craig. I'll show him I'm completely over him. I'll even be nice to Alexandra.* With that resolution, she finished dressing and went to join Cassie at breakfast.

"We're in the same group," Cassie said, greeting her and looking up from a bowl of cornflakes. "The food looks disgusting, by the way. Even worse than Rosemont. Thank heavens I'm vegetarian, because I wouldn't want to try that sausage!"

"I think I'll stick to toast," Jill said. "I didn't sleep too well last night."

Cassie eyed her critically. "You don't look too great," she said. "Meeting him again upset you more than you thought it would, didn't it?"

"Who, Craig?" Jill asked lightly. "Oh, no, it had nothing to do with him. It was just that hard cot and the wind coming in through all those cracks. Remind me never to join the army." She grabbed a couple of slices of cold toast and a packet of jelly. "So what thrilling thing awaits us today?" she asked. "Do we get to feed the great whites or tag a few sea lions with Alexandra?"

Cassie grinned. "I hate to admit it, but that girl really must be tough if she tags sea lions. Those guys are fierce, and they move fast when they want to. We have a much less dangerous assignment this morning. We're going on the tide pool walk. There's a very low tide today."

"Great," Jill said. "That sounds more my speed. I think I can handle things that live in tide pools. Maybe I'll tag a turtle."

"I hope we can handle the instructors," Cassie said, shooting Jill a knowing look. "We have both Craig and Alexandra as our section leaders. I hope you can bear watching them gaze at each other between sea urchins. I don't know if I can."

Jill looked at her friend with understanding disbelief. "Oh, Cassie," she said. "I know what you feel like. Why don't we ask to change sections and get another leader?"

"What, and miss any chance I might have to impress him?" Cassie asked. "When you're as desperate as I am, Jill, you clutch at straws."

"I hope it works out for you, Cass," Jill said kindly. "But I have a feeling that one of us is going to have to feed Alexandra to the sharks before Craig notices another girl."

Cassie grinned wickedly. "That wouldn't be the hardest task I've had to do in my life," she said. Then she paused to think. "Knowing Alexandra, however, she'd probably wrestle the shark into submission."

"And then tag it!" Jill finished delightedly. "I'm glad I've got you here, Cass," she said. "I need someone to keep things in perspective for me when Jake's not around."

"Jake's very good for you," Cassandra agreed. "He stops you from worrying and brooding too much. You definitely need someone like him in your life."

Jill sighed. "It's terrible that there is no telephone at this place. He was going to call me every evening. Now I've got to wait five more days before I talk to him again." She pushed away her plate. "Oh, well, I guess we'd better get out there and face the killer starfish!"

"Jill Gardner, there is no such thing as a killer starfish!" Cassie called as she hurried after her to join the group. Craig greeted Jill with a smile. So did Alexandra, who looked twice as lovely and delicate by daylight, with her pixie face framed by a light blue parka hood. It was a clear, cold morning, the sky an ice blue and every outline sharp as if it had been etched in glass. The ocean spray sparkled as it caught rays of sun and seemed to hang for a moment, suspended above the rocks, while sea gulls swooped through it. *Like parting a lace curtain*, Jill thought. She stood for a moment, admiring the beauty of the scene.

I'd like to sit up here on the hillside and write a poem about it, she decided. *That would be a much better idea than tripping through the tide pools.*

"Are you ready to go?"

Jill was startled from her thoughts at the sound of Craig's voice, annoyed that he still had the power to make her react like that. He waved his hand to beckon the group forward. The walk wound down the trail, through the scrub, across some slippery rocks, and out to the tide pools. They took up positions, and Craig started explaining what they were to look for. At the first pool, everyone could see the sea anemone except Jill. She felt like a fool and kept quiet.

Cassandra was already in her element, asking intelligent questions and pointing out differences between types of algae on the rocks. The rest of the group seemed to know what they were talking about, too. Jill felt as if she were a visitor from another planet. She found herself longing to do something clever so that Craig would notice her again.

She stared with determination into the next pool and noticed with a thrill that a small snail was scuttling rapidly across the bottom of it. Even Jill, with her limited knowledge of biology, was sure that snails were supposed to move slowly. "Look at the unusual snail," she called. The rest of the group clustered around, peering into the unsettled water. "Where?" somebody asked.

"Just by that big clump of seaweed." Jill pointed. "Can't you see that conical shell?"

"Oh, that?" the boy next to her asked scornfully. "That's not a snail."

"Oh?" Jill asked, confused. She had thought that things with curly shells on their backs were snails, and this thing certainly possessed a curly shell.

"That's just a hermit crab," Craig said kindly. "He's just borrowing a snail shell."

"Oh," Jill said again.

"Didn't you notice the legs?" the boy beside her asked. "They should have given you a clue. You don't meet too many snails with legs."

Jill heard Alexandra give her shrill little laugh. She turned away and hurried off across the seaweed after Craig. "I didn't want to take this stupid course anyway," she muttered to herself. She felt her left foot slithering across the slippery surface. She struggled to regain her balance. "Watch out!" somebody yelled at her. She stepped backward and felt herself sliding, into a deep, cold pool.

"Oh, oh, drowning victim!" someone shouted.

"Quick, get the lifeguards," one boy yelled, laughing.

"I get to do the mouth-to-mouth!" his friend quipped.

Jill tried to climb up the seaweed draped

sides of the pool. The icy water was up to her thighs. She could feel her cheeks flaming red with embarrassment. Warm hands finally grasped her and dragged her out.

"Maybe she wanted to do some closer observation!" somebody said, and again Jill heard Alexandra laugh.

"It's not funny," the boy who had mocked her earlier said as she stood, teeth chattering, wishing the ground would swallow her up. "She's disturbed the whole ecology of that tide pool. It's useless now from our point of view."

"I think you'd better go straight back and change," Craig said, eyeing her seriously. "It's very cold today. I'd like to remind the rest of you to walk very carefully across these rocks. The seaweed is slippery. Okay, follow me. We're just coming to the pool where we saw the lobster last time." He turned and marched ahead of the group as if he'd completely put Jill from his mind.

THIRTEEN

Long after Jill had dried and changed, she stayed inside the cabin. Under no circumstances would she clamber down over those rocks and join the group again. She felt angry at the whole world—at the snickering boy for his smart aleck remarks, at Alexandra for laughing at them, and at Craig for treating her like just another student. Most of all, though, she was angry at herself. "How could I have done such a dumb thing?" she said aloud as she savagely brushed the tangles from her hair. "And why should it worry me so much? Why should I care what any of them thinks? They mean nothing to me. Even Craig— why should it matter to me what he thinks anymore?" But it did matter. Jill knew it as she finished brushing her hair and swept it off her face with two combs. It mattered very much to her that Craig now thought she was an idiot and that Alexandra had laughed at her.

"It will not happen again," she vowed. "I will make sure I keep out of their way for the rest of this week."

But keeping out of Craig and Alexandra's way was not going to be so easy. Since Jill had been assigned to their group, she had to meet with them several times daily or fail the week's assignments. She thought about requesting a change, but Cassie so obviously wanted to be around Craig and so obviously wanted Jill with her that Jill knew she would have to stick with the original group.

That first afternoon passed harmlessly enough in the lab, even though Jill had never been good at using a microscope. Usually the specimen she was supposed to be studying looked like a wiggling, shapeless blur to her.

The evening passed smoothly, as well, with a long slide presentation during which most of the students fell asleep. Jill only turned around once to see Alexandra with her head on Craig's shoulder. *I wish I could call Jake*, she thought.

The next morning her group was scheduled to spend the day in a boat observing sea mammals.

"It looks like a very small boat to me," Jill commented to Cassie as they walked down to the dock together. "Are you sure boats that size are seaworthy?"

"It's fine," Cassie said. "I was out in it a couple of times before. Besides, look how calm the water is today."

Jill watched the waves crashing onto the rocks beside the jetty and did not think it looked at all calm.

"I can't wait," Cassie said, climbing into the boat ahead of Jill. "There's been a pod of dolphins sighted in the area, and this is a good time of year for whales."

"Oh, wonderful," Jill muttered. "I always wanted to play Moby Dick. What happens if a whale comes up under a boat this size? We'll be eaten for breakfast."

Cassie shook her head in disbelief. "What you know about biology would fit on a postage stamp," she said. "The gray whales along this coast eat tiny organisms, not people."

"But what about the killer whales?" Jill asked. "They didn't get their name from munching on seaweed."

"We're not about to meet a killer whale," Cassie said. "They're mostly farther north. Of course, there are times when they follow the seal population down here."

"Somehow," Jill said dryly, "I don't find your answer very comforting."

Cassie laughed. "Whales are very intelligent," she said. "Why would they bother with humans?"

"I've seen the movie," Jill said. "You know, the killer whale that takes revenge because somebody shot its mate? It goes around tearing up boats and eating the people in them."

Cassie snorted. "So you also believed that Godzilla destroyed Tokyo?" she asked.

The boat had filled with students. Jill found herself on a bench against the railing. "Great! We get the best view," Cassie whispered to her. Jill wished she had taken one of the inside seats when she had the chance. The foamy green waves looked uncomfortably close. Craig signaled to the skipper, and the boat's motor started up with a deep, vibrating chug. The boat gradually moved away from its dock. It bumped and shuddered over the choppy surface, water slapping over the sides as the boat met each wave. Jill pulled up her parka hood and cowered against Cassie.

The boat pulled away from the shore until the cabins looked like doll houses perched on a papier-mâché cliff. Jill's stomach lurched as the bow of the boat rose and fell. Beyond where the waves broke, the bumping was replaced with a slow, heavy rolling motion that took an even worse toll on her stomach. The boat cruised quietly up and down the coast, as the group patiently waited but saw nothing except a few sea birds. While the others kept a sharp lookout on the water's surface, Jill riveted her eyes on the rail, willing her stomach to stop fighting the rhythm of the ocean.

"Keep looking hard," Craig told the group. "I'm sure we'll spot something soon."

I hope I'm not going to disgrace myself and be sick, Jill thought as she attempted to look at the bobbing coastline. She imagined Alexandra and Craig complaining about the disruption of the ecology while she lost her toast over the side of the boat. *I will not be sick*, she thought determinedly. *I will use my willpower to fight it off. Mind over matter!* She braced herself against the side of the boat and stared grimly down at the water.

"Are you feeling okay?" Cassie asked. "Your face has turned a wild shade of green."

"I'll survive," Jill muttered.

"You want me to take you in the cabin so you can lie down?" Cassie asked.

Jill shook her head. "I am not giving that girl the satisfaction of watching me collapse," she said. "Look at her. How can anyone be so horribly healthy?"

Alexandra was kneeling up in the prow of the boat. With her blond hair streaming behind her, she looked like a mermaid. Her cheeks were glowing as she turned to laugh and say something to Craig. Craig himself seemed to be glowing with health, his face deeply tan against his off-white turtleneck. "He looks like a commercial for some men's cologne," Jill commented.

Cassie nodded. "He is so cute," she said. "I wish a large wave would break over the bow of the boat and wash Alexandra overboard."

"Then Craig would only dive in to save her," Jill said. "I think you'd better face it, Cassie. The time isn't quite right for you and Craig."

"It sure seems that way," Cassie said. "Life isn't fair, is it? Why didn't you introduce me to him when you two were just breaking up? Then you could have passed him straight to me."

Jill laughed a little uneasily. "I don't know if I would have been unselfish enough to do that, Cass."

"But I thought you wanted to break up?"

Jill stared thoughtfully out to sea. "The way things were going, it was best for both of us," she said.

"But it's all over now, and I have Jake, and he has what's-her-name. Let's not talk about it anymore."

Roger, another T.A., walked past them. "You two should be watching, not gabbing," he said. "You might miss something."

"What is there to miss?" Jill asked. "All we've seen so far is waves."

"You never can tell," Roger said. "Who knows what might be lurking in the depths, right, Cassandra?"

Cassandra responded with a smile as he continued down the deck.

"He knows your name?" Jill asked.

Cassandra shrugged her shoulders. "He was here over the holidays, too. We went out looking for starfish a few times."

Jill turned her gaze back toward the heaving ocean and noticed a small fountain of spray. She was about to call out that she'd seen something when she remembered the embarrassment of the hermit crab. Maybe small fountains of spray were common. About a minute later someone else yelled. "There's one, over there! Look at him blow!"

"What is it?" Jill asked Cassandra, as everyone leaped up to the railing.

"It's a whale," Cassandra said excitedly. "See? That jet of water is from his blowhole."

Jill was angry that she had missed the opportunity to be the first whale sighter. She imagined Craig admiring her good eyes and Alexandra looking on, annoyed. But it was too late now. The boat surged forward toward the last jet of water. The entire group was pressed against one side of the rail to peer out at the water. Even Jill forgot her seasickness. She knelt beside Cassie on the rail side bench and looked down into the green water.

"Whales always surface three times in quick succession then make one deep dive," Roger told them. "So we're hurrying ahead to try to guess where he's going to come up again."

The skipper cut the engine, and the boat began to drift. Everyone gripped the rail and stared silently at the empty waters.

"Maybe he won't come up if he sees the boat here," someone behind Jill suggested.

Then suddenly there was a noise like a giant sigh just beside the boat. A jet of water spouted up. A sleek gray back broke the surface. Then an enormous tail, encrusted with barnacles and wide as the boat itself, reared out of the water. Somebody behind Jill screamed and grabbed her shoulder. The tail splashed down, sending up a shower of spray. Everyone moved at once, and to her horror, Jill felt herself being pushed forward and over the side of the boat. She heard Cassandra yell her name and she made a frantic grab at the railing. Then she hit the icy water with a splash.

Water so cold that it took her breath away was everywhere. She fought for air not even knowing which way was up. She could feel the water inside her parka, flooding her clothing, dragging her down. Then she remembered the whale. For a few seconds she stopped struggling and let herself just drop down, too frightened to move. Nobody had said what kind of whale it was. What if it wasn't the kind that ate little shrimp? She could almost feel the great gray shape brushing against her, huge teeth taking hold of her. She gave a mighty kick upward.

As her head broke the surface, she saw a figure poised on the prow, throwing off his jacket before preparing to dive. "Hang on, Jill, I'm coming!" Craig yelled. He plunged into the water and came up beside her, encircling her with strong arms, holding her tightly.

"Craig," she gasped. "Don't let go of me!"

"Don't worry," he said, his icy cheek touching hers. "I'm not going to let go of you again."

FOURTEEN

A line landed in the water beside them. Craig reached for it, and they were dragged back toward the boat. Everything seemed to be happening in slow motion to Jill, as in a dream when she would try to move but found her limbs as heavy as lead. She was in the middle of a dream now, with Craig whispering gently to her, the way he had in so many dreams of the past. She was dimly conscious of hands reaching out for her, grabbing at her, and lifting her up. She was aware of being carried down steep steps, of people undressing her and wrapping her in blankets. Vaguely she wondered whether she should let strange people remove her wet clothes and whether the strange people were male or female. But she was too drowsy and too comfortable to worry.

She heard Craig say, "Here, drink this."

"What is it?" she muttered.

"Don't ask, just swallow," came the command, and Jill swallowed something that was so fiery, it took her breath away. But shortly afterward her toes and fingers began to obey her again.

"Now you just lie there until you warm up," Craig told her.

"You better get your own clothes changed pretty quickly." Another male voice spoke from far away.

"I'll be fine." Craig's voice was right beside her. "I've got to make sure she's okay first."

A wonderful warmth was spreading upward from Jill's toes. "Everything's fine," she murmured to herself. "Everything's just right."

When she opened her eyes, the first thing she noticed was a lantern swinging above her head. She lay wondering what was making the lantern swing until she made sense of the *thud-thudding* of a deep motor, the creaking of wood, and the slap of water. Then she remembered where she was. She opened her eyes fully and was starting to sit up when she realized she was wrapped only in blankets. As her eyes moved around the room, she noticed that Craig was curled up in a blanket on a bunk opposite her. Jill gathered the blankets around her. Craig turned his head toward her at the sound of her movement and smiled.

"How are you feeling?" he asked.

"Fine, I think," she murmured, suddenly shy with him. "My fingers and toes all seem to work again."

"That's great," he said. "I was worried about you. People don't survive long in an ocean as cold as this."

"You dived in to save me," Jill said, gazing at him. "I've never, ever, been so scared in my life. Thank you for saving me."

"My pleasure," Craig said, grinning at her.

Jill felt herself blushing. "I feel like such a fool," she said. "First the tide pool and now this. You must think I've turned into an idiot who spends her time falling into things. I bet you're glad you don't have to put up with me anymore."

Craig looked at her steadily. "I wouldn't say that," he said. He got up and crossed over to her. "It's funny," he said unsteadily, "I thought I'd completely gotten over you. But when I saw you fall into that water, I'd have knocked anybody out of the way to get to you. Anybody! I hadn't realized—"

He sank down beside her, taking her hand. "I hadn't realized," he said again slowly, "how much you mean to me." He pulled her toward him, and suddenly, before Jill could do anything, he was kissing her hungrily.

The thought that kissing Craig might be unwise flashed quickly through Jill's mind, but as Craig's lips crushed against hers and his arms wrapped around her, she found herself kissing him as fervently as he was kissing her.

"Very interesting," came a crisp voice behind them. "This must be a new method of mouth-to-mouth!" Craig and Jill broke apart to see Alexandra and Cassandra standing on the steps, watching them. Alexandra looked as cool and lovely as ever, but her eyes were angry. "You must teach me sometime, Craig," she said. "It looks more interesting than the old method."

Jill pulled the blanket up over her bare shoulder.

"We came down to see if you'd woken up yet," Cassandra said awkwardly, her own cheeks flaming.

"And she most certainly has," Alexandra said.

"How are you feeling?" Cassandra asked.

"I'd say she was feeling just great," Alexandra answered for her. Jill felt Craig's hands stiffen as he held her.

"Cut it out, Alexandra," he said.

For what seemed an eternity nobody moved, nobody spoke. Then Cassandra said, "I'll see you up on deck, Jill," and turned and walked back up the stairs.

"And I'll see you back up on deck, Alexandra," Craig said firmly. Alexandra didn't say another word, but turned and stomped back up the iron steps, too. Craig and Jill sat looking at each other, then they both burst out laughing.

"That was one of life's most embarrassing moments, wasn't it?" he asked at last.

Jill nodded. "But not as embarrassing as falling into the ocean in front of a whole boatload of people. I don't know how I can face them again."

"It's not the first time it's happened," Craig said. "In fact, I fell in from an open boat when we were following some dolphin last year. So you're not the only one."

"You never told me about it!" Jill said, her eyes teasing his.

Craig looked slightly embarrassed. "No, well, it's not the sort of thing you phone home about!"

A new thought flashed through Jill's mind: *Jake would have called me about it instantly. He'd have said, "Guess what? I just fell off a boat!" and then he would have roared with laughter.* Jill looked up at Craig. "I guess you'd better go back up to the others," she said. "Who knows what rumors Alexandra might be spreading about us?"

Craig shrugged his shoulders. "Let her," he said. "It doesn't worry me."

"Or worse still," Jill said, "she might come

down in person and tag you. I'm sure you don't weigh as much as a sea lion!"

Craig flashed her a knowing look. "Do I detect a note of jealousy?" he asked.

"Not at all," Jill said. "I just feel threatened by girls who can do everything and look gorgeous at the same time."

Craig grinned. "She is a little overpowering, isn't she?" he asked.

Jill nodded. "But definitely gorgeous," she said.

"So you are jealous," Craig said, teasing her. "It's very good for my ego to have two women fighting over me."

"There was never anything wrong with your ego, Craig," Jill said firmly. "And let me tell you that I am not jealous. I have definitely gotten over you, and she is welcome to you!"

Craig smiled, his eyes holding Jill's. "I didn't notice you pushing me away when I kissed you just now."

"That was for old times' sake," Jill said.

Craig's smile broadened. "I see," he said.

Jill looked around nervously and noticed the coastline moving up and down outside the porthole. "You'd better go up on deck, Craig," she said, "and give me a chance to get some clothes on before we dock."

Craig followed her gaze out the window.

"You're right," he said. "But nothing of yours will be dry enough yet. I'll go grab Roger's parka for you. It'll be big enough to reach down to your knees."

"I'll feel like a fool—" Jill began, but Craig laughed.

"Better than walking out wrapped only in a blanket," he said. "I'll go get the parka." He turned back to look at her. "Don't go away," he whispered. Then he ran up the steps, leaving Jill feeling utterly confused.

FIFTEEN

"Very elegant. Is that the latest in seagoing fashion?" Cassandra asked as Jill finally emerged from the cabin and climbed off the boat and onto the dock. Jill pulled the parka more tightly around her. "Not you too, please," she said. "I've had enough cracks from Alexandra."

Cassandra grinned. "You should have seen her face when she came up from the cabin," she said. "If looks could kill, they'd have been taking you out of this boat in a little pine box."

"And are you mad at me, too?" Jill asked as the girls continued to walk up to the cabins. "You looked kind of mad."

Cassandra shook her head. "I was embarrassed," she said. "I've led a sheltered life. I'm just not used to coming into cabins and seeing X-rated scenes being played."

"It was not X-rated," Jill said, her cheeks flaming. "Craig was merely happy I was all right again, and he kissed me—for old times' sake."

Cassandra laughed. "If that was for old times, I'd hate to see what the new times are like." Then she reached out toward Jill. "It's okay," she said. "I guess I'm jealous. I just wish it had been me that fell in instead of you. But then Craig probably wouldn't have bothered to dive in to save me. He would have watched from the deck as the whale swallowed me. And he certainly wouldn't have kissed me if I'd come to life again." She turned to look at Jill critically. "So does that mean you two are back together? It certainly looks like it."

Jill sighed. "I don't know, Cassie," she said. "It all happened so fast. I didn't mean to kiss him; it just happened. And now I don't know anything. I used to be so much in love with him. If he had phoned from the North Pole and said, 'Get up here fast,' I'd have run all the way. I don't think you get over love like that in a hurry. But I don't know if I want to start it all up again. I don't know if he does, either. Maybe it was just a spur of the moment kiss for both of us. After all, we had both been through a traumatic experience."

Cassandra shook her head. "I don't know if I should be glad about it or not. It did have the effect of making Craig mad at Alexandra, which is good, but now I have two of you to fight off! Oh, well, there never was really much hope for me, was there?"

Jill smiled kindly. "It's tough falling in love with the wrong person. Believe me, I know. Remember the crush I had on Ryan? Come to think of it, love is tough, period. Especially the breaking-up part of it. I've already gone through it once with Craig. And Jake is so special. I don't think I want to complicate my life again. Oh, I wish I'd never taken this crummy course. All I've learned is that the Pacific Ocean is very cold in February and that whales' tails make large splashes. Now I want a hot shower, and all they have here is a warm trickle."

"I'm going right in to lunch," Cassandra said. "I'm dying of starvation, and they actually make great avocado and alfalfa sprout sandwiches here. See you in a while, okay?" She waved to Jill and turned toward the cafeteria. Jill continued up the winding path toward the cabins and pushed open her rickety front door. She had already dropped her wet clothes in a pile on the floor beside her bed and opened her suitcase to look for clean clothes before noticing an unfamiliar object lying on top of her sleeping bag. It was a long white cardboard box. As Jill picked it up, she could see pink roses through the cellophane lid. She tore it open and picked up the card. Scribbled in Jake's almost illegible handwriting was, "I miss you already, I'm going crazy with no phone, so I had to send these with a kindly passing salmon. If you want me to come and rescue you from killer jellyfish, just find another salmon who is coming upstream and give a message to him. I'll be waiting by the river to grab it! Yours forever, Jake."

Jill felt her eyes misting over as she stood gazing down at the roses. *What a stupid, crazy, sweet thing to do*, she thought. *I'm so lucky to have someone like him. Why did I have to find Craig again and complicate everything?*

In the shower she tried to analyze her feelings about Craig. She remembered how her heart had beat fast when she saw him again, how jealous she had been when he stood close to Alexandra, how good his lips felt when he kissed her. She remembered, too, what it had been like when they had been in love. Maybe that love had never died. Maybe it was only sleeping. Was it worth reawakening? But wasn't her feeling for Jake just as strong? Would she always wonder, no matter what she did, if she had given up the right boy?

The solution to her dilemma did not become any clearer when she dried her hair, nor when she went to the cafeteria and grabbed one of the last sandwiches left. She only learned that she was not hungry and the bread tasted like cardboard. She walked out of the cafeteria and threw half the sandwich to the sea gulls. They swooped down, crying and screeching at each other, fighting for it. Jill watched them passively.

"I can't believe you wasted that delicious bologna," Craig's voice said gently behind her. She turned to face him.

"I didn't feel much like eating," she said.

"Me, neither," he said. "And the bologna was disgusting. You want to come for a walk?"

Jill looked around at the camp. "What about the afternoon session?" she asked. "Shouldn't we be there? Don't you have to help run it?"

"It's only a movie," Craig said. "On whales. I think you're already an expert, don't you? Anyway, it's very dark in there. I don't think either of us would be missed, and I would like to talk to you."

"Okay, I guess," Jill said. "Maybe we should talk."

"I know a beautiful spot on the cliff up there," Craig said. "Up this path."

He turned and started to walk up a hill, his feet swishing through the short grass. Jill followed him, walking in his footsteps, both of them silent. When the Wildlife Center was far below them, Craig fell into step beside her. "You know," he said seriously, "you have really complicated my life, showing up like this."

"I have?" Jill asked uneasily.

Craig nodded. "I thought that I was completely over you—we were all done and forgotten, a piece of my history. But when I saw you again, I realized that getting over somebody isn't that easy. I can't help thinking about you, Jill."

"I feel the same way," Jill said.

"You do?" Craig asked hopefully. He turned toward her. "So what do we do now?" he asked.

Jill shrugged her shoulders uneasily. "I wish I knew," she said. "I don't know if we made a mistake in breaking up. I thought it was a wise thing to do. The gradual drifting apart was so painful for me—wondering if you were with another girl, wondering if you still felt anything for me."

Craig took her hand. His own was firm and warm. "It was painful for me, too, Jill," he said. "But I just couldn't go on any longer. It wasn't that I stopped feeling anything for you. Just the opposite, in fact."

"What do you mean?" Jill asked.

Craig stopped walking and stood turned away, looking out toward the ocean, as if he didn't want to face her. "I realized how involved we were both getting," he said. "We'd been going together for more than a year, and we'd started talking about the future, with a capital F. Suddenly I felt very trapped. I realized that if I stayed with you any longer it would lead to a serious commitment. I also realized that I wasn't ready to think about the future and marriage. I didn't want to be tied down. And yet I knew it wasn't fair to you to expect you to be a casual girlfriend."

He turned and looked at her, his eyes pleading with her to understand. She nodded. "I felt the same way, Craig," she said.

His eyes opened wider. "You did?" he asked.

She smiled at his astonishment. "That's right. The first few weeks of college I began to ask myself if I wanted to be tied to a guy who was a hundred miles away when everyone else was going out and having fun. College should be a time for meeting lots of people and dating lots of guys. Maybe it would have been different if we'd both been at the same college and had seen each other every day. But then maybe we would have felt smothered and broken up. Who can say?"

"But you still do feel something for me?" he asked hesitantly.

Jill nodded. "I think I'll always love you a little."

He turned toward her and took her hands in his. "But you don't want to try again right now?"

"I don't know if it would be wise right now, Craig," Jill said. "We've both been through the pain of breaking up. Now we've both moved on. You've got someone new and so have I."

"You have?" he interrupted.

"And he's very special, Craig," she said.

"Very long-term special?"

"I don't know yet. I think I'm a bit young to talk about long-term. All I can say is that I'm really happy with him right now."

"I see," Craig said. He continued to look at her.

"You have Alexandra," she said.

Craig smiled. "Definitely not long-term," he said firmly. "Sometimes I find a girl who can do everything better than me a little scary."

Jill laughed. "Oh, Craig," she said. "I wish love weren't so complicated. I bet the moment I get back to Rosemont, I'll start wishing I'd never left you."

"Then don't," he said.

"But you just said yourself that you don't want a long-term commitment yet," Jill said patiently. "It wouldn't be right for either of us to tie the other one down. And we couldn't just agree to a casual relationship."

"You're right as usual," Craig said. "I wish you hadn't fallen into that ocean. My emotions were under control until then. I have enough class work to worry about without having two girls on my mind!"

Jill laughed suddenly. "That was what Cassie said. You remember my roommate, Cassandra?"

"The dark one I pulled off the rock? You two are a pair of menaces, aren't you?"

"She happens to be crazy about you."

"About me?"

Jill nodded. "She has the biggest crush on you."

"That's very funny," Craig said.

"Not for her, poor girl," Jill answered.

"No, I didn't mean funny—ha, ha—I meant funny, as in strange, because my roommate, Roger, has the biggest crush on her."

"Roger?" Jill said. "The Roger from the ship today? The Roger whose parka I was wearing?"

"That's right. But he's so shy. He's been bugging me to find a way to get him and Cassandra together."

Jill started to laugh. "But Cassie had no idea," she said. "Aren't people strange? We all go around falling in love with the wrong person at the wrong time. Wait until I tell Cassie about this! Maybe a Roger in the hand will be worth a lost Craig in the bush."

Craig slipped his arms around her waist. "I'll miss you," he said.

"I'll miss you, too," she whispered.

"May I kiss you once more, for old times' sake?"

Jill laughed. "As long as it's not as X-rated as the last old times' sake kiss."

He pulled her toward him. "Just a friendly kiss to remember you by," he whispered as his lips came to meet hers.

The kiss lasted a long while. As they drew apart, he smiled down at her. "Will you make a date with me for four years from today?" he asked.

Jill nodded, her eyes smiling at him. "Four years from today," she said.

Craig reached inside his back pocket and pulled out a small book. "Five-year diary," he said solemnly. "You never know when you might need it." He thumbed through and slipped out a slender, gold pen. "Here we are," he said, flipping through the pages of the calendar. "Date with Jill. Shall we say twelve for lunch, or would you rather make it dinner?"

Jill looked at him and started laughing. "Definitely dinner," she said. "Much more romantic."

SIXTEEN

"It seems strange to be back in the old routine, doesn't it?" Cassandra asked Jill as they walked to class on Monday morning. "It felt like we were away for much more than a week."

Jill nodded. "It was like being in a time warp," she said, "being totally cut off from the rest of the world like that."

Cassandra raised an eyebrow. "Some of us were not totally cut off," she said. "Some of us had roses with strange messages on them arriving every few minutes."

"It was not every few minutes," Jill said, grinning. "You didn't do too badly yourself, once you and Roger started talking about starfish."

Cassandra swept back her long black hair. "Roger is very nice," she said. "I enjoy talking to him. Unfortunately he does not send shivers up and down my spine every time I think of him."

"That's always the way," Jill agreed. "The boys who are nice, and available, and right for us are not usually the ones who make us weak at the knees."

"Some of us, of course, have more than our share," Cassandra said severely. "I wish I'd had the chance to choose between Jake and Craig."

"You don't really," Jill said. She paused while Cassandra adjusted the mountain of books she was carrying. "But there really was not much of a choice to make," Jill said. "I could tell Craig really didn't want to get back together. His emotions were all upside-down after he rescued me. Mine were, too, especially seeing him with another girl. But I realize now it's just the memory that I still love. I was longing to get back to Jake. Wasn't it sweet of him to send those flowers?"

"Very sweet," Cassandra said. "I gather he was pleased to see you last night, judging by the time you came back to our room."

"Were you awake that late?" Jill grinned sheepishly. "As a matter of fact, we sat and talked for three hours, honestly talked, Cass. I told him everything about the week, and we laughed so much."

"Even about Craig?"

"Even about Craig," Jill said. "He understood exactly what I'd been feeling. He's so easy to talk to, Cassie. Sometimes I feel I've known him all my life. I really think our relationship has changed. At first I thought he was attractive and exciting, but I wasn't sure of myself around him. Now I feel so comfortable with him. I can tell him anything, or I can even sit beside him without saying a thing. That's a good feeling."

"I'm envious again," Cassandra said. "Have you had a chance to check your mailbox yet?"

Jill smiled. "I had other things to do last night," she said, "which shows how well we've settled in now. The first weeks of college I ran to my mailbox every day."

They pushed open the door into the administration building and found their boxes in the mailroom. "A letter from my mother, ugh!" Cassandra said, eyeing the elegant printed envelope. "Probably to tell me to come home for some party or to meet some nice boy she wants to fix me up with."

"I've got a letter from my mother, too," Jill said. "I wonder if she's heard anything about Toni."

"It's so strange you haven't heard a thing from her since you left her that night," Cassandra said.

Jill shook her head. "I know, and I'm so worried, Cass. We've had fights before, but Toni has never shut me out of her life for so long."

"But you told her you wanted nothing more

to do with her until she left those weirdos," Cassandra reminded her.

"I know," Jill said uneasily. "But I didn't really think it'd take so long. I kept hoping that she'd get tired of them sooner. I guess I really have lost her this time."

"It may take time," Cassie said kindly. "After all, her life fell to pieces when Brandt left her. Maybe she still needs a strong support group."

"But not like those people, Cass," Jill said. "I've read about cults. They brainwash people. They never let them leave."

Cassandra put a restraining hand on Jill's arm. "Hey, wait a minute, Jill. You're talking about Toni. I only met her for a few days but even I could tell that she isn't the sort of person you could brainwash in a hurry. And you know nothing about this group she's joined except that they dress funny and go out collecting money. Well, I wear weird clothes, and I often go out raising money for my pet causes. But that doesn't make me a bad person, does it? You like having me for a friend?"

"But these people were different, Cass," Jill tried to explain. "It was the chanting and the silly grins they all had on their faces. I wish I knew what to do to reach Toni. I wonder what her parents think about it. Do you think I should get in touch with them, so we could plan something together?"

"What sort of something?" Cassandra asked uneasily.

"To rescue her and bring her back to the real world," Jill said.

Cassandra frowned. "I don't think Toni would take kindly to being rescued," she said. "You've got to let her lead her own life, Jill. And don't worry so much. I'm sure it will all turn out for the best."

"I wish I could believe that," Jill said. "But Toni's been my best friend since second grade. I can't let her down now."

They walked across the rain-soaked grass toward the natural sciences building, opening the letters from home and reading silently as they walked.

"Yuck." Cassandra broke the silence first. "My mother says the country club is forming a junior golf section. How could she ever expect me to play junior golf!"

"My mother had her first real day in court last week," Jill said proudly. "The judge asked for some reference materials, and my mother had to look them up for the attorney. How exciting! She says she was scared silly while the judge waited for her to go through her files, but the attorney was pleased she found them so quickly. How about that!"

"Oh, no!" Cassandra exclaimed, turning the page. "She wants us all to go to Palm Springs for spring vacation. Palm Springs! Imagine. Plastic palm trees and geriatric golfers."

"Oh, no!" Jill exclaimed. "Listen, what did I tell you? My mother says, 'Have you heard anything from Toni recently? Her parents are a bit worried about her because she's left her apartment and moved in with some strange people. They haven't heard from her for a while now, and she doesn't have a phone where they can reach her.' See? That's what cults do. They cut you off from your family. I wish I could go to Seattle and do something!"

"There really is nothing you can do," Cassandra said firmly. "If Toni doesn't want you to interfere, you can't. The best thing you can do is wait patiently until she decides to get in touch with you again."

"That's so hard, Cassie," Jill said. "But I can't think of anything to do."

They reached the natural sciences building just as light rain began to fall.

"We were so lucky to get a good week out on the coast," Cassandra remarked. "We couldn't have collected many specimens in the rain, and now we have hundreds of slides to go through. I can't wait."

Jill shook her head in amazement. "I can't imagine anyone being excited about looking at squirmy things under microscopes," she said. "I wish you were my lab partner. I can never get the horrible thing into focus."

"We science majors have to work harder than you humanities people," Cassie said. "It doesn't really matter if you mix up an elephant seal with algae, but we mustn't even mistake one type of alga for another. Anyway, you've got Terrence in your group. He'll help you."

Jill made a face. "I don't know if I want to give Terrence the opportunity to put his face close to mine beside the microscope. It might give him ideas again. But you're right. He does seem to know what he's doing, which is more than I do. And I don't really know anyone else in my section."

Terrence waved a big, friendly hand as he saw Jill come into the room.

"I got here first and stole the easiest slides for us," he said, beaming at her. "Even we'll be able to identify these, I think."

Jill put down her books on the shelf beside him. "I can tell the difference between a crab and a jellyfish after last week's outing, but don't count on any more than that."

"Did it go well?" Terrence asked. "I was so mad I was sick and couldn't go. I hear the weather was terrific and you saw a real whale close up."

"Much too close for me," Jill said, smiling. "I fell off the boat right beside it."

Terrence's eyes opened wide. "Was that you?" he asked. "I heard that somebody fell in and some guy made a dramatic rescue."

"That was me," Jill said, looking down at her notes.

"And who was the guy?"

There was a pause. "Someone I used to know," Jill said at length.

"Oh," Terrence said. He coughed uneasily. "Here. We ought to get started. Let's try this one first."

Jill watched as he slipped in the first piece of glass and peered down into the microscope. His longish sandy-colored hair flopped forward over his boyish face, and he pushed it back with a characteristically quick gesture. Jill smiled at him fondly. *I really like Terrence, but it's sad that I could never love him.*

It was almost as if Terrence had been reading her mind. He looked up suddenly and grinned at her. "You just missed an amoeba dividing in two. It made me think how very lucky amoebas are. They have such an easy life. They have no problems about being male or female or falling in love."

Jill nodded with understanding. "Would you rather just split in two one day?" she asked.

"It certainly would make life a lot less complicated," Terrence agreed. "Look how much time and energy humans waste on falling in love, most of the time with the wrong people." He looked back down at the slide again.

He's right, Jill thought. *Terrence still thinks about me; my life was all mixed up between Craig and Jake; Cassie was dreaming about Craig when all the time Roger was dreaming about Cassie. What a crazy merry-go-round.* She looked down at Terrence's head, his hair still flopping forward into his eyes. "So have you decided you'd rather be an amoeba?" she asked.

Terrence's eyes met hers. "I guess it would be pretty boring," he admitted. "You'd never wake up in the morning hoping that something exciting would happen. Your heart would never beat faster when you saw another amoeba coming your way. At least we know we're alive. I guess it's worth putting up with the times when love goes wrong, isn't it?"

Jill nodded. "Being in love is a big pain, but there are special moments in life that make it all worth it. You know, the moment when you suddenly realize that it's not just a crush any-more—that the other person doesn't just make your heart beat faster, he makes you feel all warm inside. As if you've finally come home."

Terrence looked up at her steadily. "Are you telling me that's how you feel about Jake?"

Jill paused for a moment, surprised by the question. "Yes," she said at last. "I think I am."

SEVENTEEN

March 8

Just back from a very busy weekend. Someone has donated an old barn to our group, and we are trying to get it in shape for a real summer season of theater. Spent two exhausting days moving timber and fixing leaks in a roof. Hundreds of blisters, but lots of fun, too. These guys are really crazy— sometimes a little too crazy for me. The noise level is always so high that I find myself longing for more privacy. After my own apartment, I need more space to myself. But I also need people around to stop me from thinking too much. Maybe after the summer I'll get out on my own again, but acting in a real theater will be such a great experience. Who knows, maybe Robert Redford will be driving past and get a flat tire and peep inside and discover me! Dream on, Toni! At least I *am* dreaming again, and I suppose that's a good sign. I didn't think I'd ever want to think about the future again, and I still get all choked up inside when I think of Brandt, but I've trained myself to think of him less and less. He hasn't even phoned or written once, so I know it really is all over. For weeks I kept hoping he was missing me and he'd change his mind.

Still nothing from Jill. I guess she really meant it about not wanting to talk to me until I left the group. I still can't understand why she is behaving like this. Maybe she was jealous that I have new friends, but that doesn't seem like Jill. I miss her. Maybe I should write to her. I don't want to lose her forever. If I could only persuade her to come to meet everybody. I'm sure she'd like them. I think I *will* write to her. After all, best friends don't come along too often, and we've been best friends for too long to end our friendship over a silly fight. Imagine Toni Redmond making the first move to end a fight. I really have grown up recently, haven't I?

Jill picked up her mail Friday on the way over to lunch and looked with interest at the picture postcard of the Eiffel Tower, wondering who would be writing to her from Paris. Then she saw Toni's bold, untidy handwriting.

I found this postcard in a book, and it reminded me of the great times we had last summer. Don't worry about me now, because I am really enjoying myself. We are working every weekend on an old barn at the Radletts' in Appleton, Washington, across the Columbia River from you. We are converting it and plan to move out here for the summer. So all is well, Jill. Please get in touch soon.

Love, Toni

Jill stared at the postcard, her hands trembling.

"Is something wrong, Jill?" Cassandra asked, coming over to her table with a tray heaped with salad. "You look as white as a sheet."

Jill waved the postcard. "It's from Toni," she said.

Cassandra looked puzzled. "But that should make you happy, hearing from her again."

Jill shook her head. "She's still with that group, and they're moving out to a country property for the summer," she said. "You know how cults take everyone out to a ranch and nobody leaves."

"Did Toni say that?" Cassandra asked.

Jill handed her the postcard. Cassandra shook her head as if she was trying to understand something that didn't make sense. "But, Jill, she sounds fine and happy. What are you worrying about?"

"You wouldn't understand," Jill said. "But I think that the postcard is written in code. I think she's asking for help."

"What on earth makes you think that?" Cassandra asked, still puzzled.

Jill looked up at her. "When we were in grade school we used to pass notes all the time," she said. "And when Toni was hating a class she used to write, 'I am enjoying myself today. How about you?' She also used to write in opposites. You know, she'd say, 'Isn't the teacher looking glamorous?' and, 'Don't you wish Peter would ask you out for a date?' when the teacher looked terrible, and Peter was the biggest slob in the class. I'm sure she's doing that now, Cass. She says, 'Don't worry about me,' when she really means she's in trouble and says, 'All is well,' when everything is terrible. I've got to do something, Cass."

Cassandra continued to stare at her. "Are you sure about this?" she asked. "That it's a code, I mean?"

"It's got to be," Jill said. "Why would Toni send a postcard of the Eiffel Tower? She'd phone if she wanted to talk, or she'd write a letter. No, she wrote a postcard because her mail is censored and she wants help before she has to go out there for the summer."

"So what do you plan to do?" Cassandra asked, digging her fork into a mound of sprouts and lettuce.

"I don't know. Go out there and rescue her, I suppose."

Cassandra let a smile cross her lips. "If they really are the sort of cult you think they are," she said, "how can one girl burst into their headquarters and drag away a prisoner? Or are you going to buy yourself a machine gun and a few hand grenades first?"

"You're making fun of me," Jill said angrily. "You don't even think this is serious."

Cassandra smiled again. "You're right," she said. "I think you're blowing this whole thing out of proportion. Even if Toni is part of a cult now, she sounds happy. And I don't think you should interfere."

"But the notes in school?" Jill asked. "I know she's in danger, Cass. Toni and I are so close to each other that we can sense these things. But you're right. I can't go and save her on my own. I'll ask Jake to come with me. He'll know what to do."

Cassandra stared after Jill as she ran from the cafeteria leaving an untouched hamburger on her tray.

Jill eventually tracked Jake down in the newspaper office. He was in the middle of an earnest discussion with Russel, the editor, when Jill burst in.

"Oh, there you are," she said, panting. "I've been looking for you everywhere! This was the last place I could think of."

Jake's eyes lit up. "I know you find it hard to keep away from me," he said in his deep, smooth voice, "but I never thought you'd pursue me like this!"

"It's not a joking matter, Jake," Jill pleaded. "I need to speak to you right now."

Jake looked from Jill to Russel and back again. He rose to his feet. "I guess we'd better finish up our discussion later," he said.

Jill began to feel foolish, standing there. A sudden vivid memory of the first grade flashed into her mind, a memory of feeling sick and begging the school to call her mother, only to feel perfectly well again by the time her mother arrived. She turned to Russel. "I'm sorry to interrupt like this, but something very urgent has come up. I need Jake's help right away."

Jake took Jill's arm and led her down the hall, away from the office. "Now," he said, turning toward her, a worried frown on his face. "What's the problem?"

"It's Toni," Jill said. "I've just heard from her, and she says she's going to be moving out to a ranch with those terrible people."

Jake shrugged his shoulders. "But if she wants to go, Jill—"

"That's just it," Jill said emphatically. "I'm sure she doesn't want to go! She wrote me a postcard saying how happy she was, but I'm sure she was using the same code we used to pass notes in school. We wrote everything in opposites. I'm sure she's being forced to go to the new place and she wants me to do something."

Jake looked at her suspiciously. "Like what?"

"Like rescue her," Jill said.

Jake grinned uneasily. "And if you got there and found she doesn't want to be rescued? You could end your friendship permanently."

"It's a risk I've got to take," Jill said. "I really feel she's being held against her will, and I've got to get her away before it's too late."

Jake stared at her steadily. "You know what I think?" he said at last. "I think you've finally flipped. You can't go bursting in on people, dragging them away. Even if you wanted to, you are not strong enough to drag her away from the guards any cult would have."

"I know," Jill said in a small voice. "That's why I want you to help me. You're strong. I bet you could go in there and force them to give her up."

Jake shook his head. "No, Jill," he said. "I don't want to interfere, and I don't want you to, either. If you've made a mistake and she really wants to be with her group, then she would be mad at you. If she is being held prisoner, then it would be dangerous for us to break in on a bunch of kooks. Get in touch with her folks if you're worried. It's up to them to make the first move."

Jill looked at him uneasily. "They may not know," she began. "Toni might not have wanted them to know she was in danger. I wouldn't want to upset her dad after his heart attack."

Jake put both hands on Jill's shoulders. "Jill, listen to me," he said. "I do not want you going out there. If it's as bad as you think, it's a situation you aren't equipped to handle. I don't want you beaten up by some oversize zombies. Please promise me you won't do anything dumb."

"So you won't help me?" Jill asked, her voice quivering at the edge of a sob.

Jake looked down at her fondly. "I just don't want you to overreact," he said. "And I don't want you to take any risks."

"But if Toni really is in danger," Jill pleaded.

"Try calling her at school," Jake suggested. "You could leave a message at her college for her to call you back because you're worried. If she hasn't called in a week, then we'll drive over and take a look on a weekend, okay?"

"I guess," Jill said.

A smile creased Jake's face. "I can't believe any cult would want to kidnap Toni for more than a couple of weeks," he said. "I would have thought by now she'd have knocked over their incense and sacred idols and put her foot in their rice bowls enough times to make her public danger number one."

"You always joke about everything," Jill said, turning away from him.

"I try to look at everything realistically," Jake said. "And you worry too much. I thought I'd cured you of all that worrying. I can see I'm going to have to kidnap you and brainwash you sometime." He planted a gentle kiss on her forehead and put his arm around her as he led her from the building.

EIGHTEEN

Jill tried calling Toni's college right after lunch, only to be told by a snooty receptionist that the college administration could not pass on personal messages to students. Since she didn't know the names of any of Toni's teachers, she had to put the phone down, almost crying with frustration. All afternoon she found it impossible to concentrate on her classes, even though she had her favorite English class with Dr. Holloman. Every time she tried to concentrate on Chaucer, a picture of Toni—dressed in tattered purple robes and peering out hopefully from a locked cell—would swim before her eyes.

I've got to go and see this weekend, she decided. *If Jake won't drive me, I'll find someone else who will, or I'll rent a car myself.* In spite of her brave words, however, Jill felt sick whenever she thought about carrying out the plan. Would she ever dare to rent a car and drive into a cult's headquarters? What if they brainwashed *her*?

Jill was brooding back in her room when she heard her name being yelled down the dorm hall. She rushed to the phone and snatched it up, praying to hear Toni's voice on the other end. But, instead, a deep, familiar voice asked, "Jill? Jill Gardner?"

"Yes," she said suspiciously. "Who's this?"

"It's Brandt," the voice replied. "Brandt Caldwell. You remember me?"

"Oh, yes," Jill stammered. "I remember you. Where are you calling from?"

"From Seattle. I came up here looking for Toni, and now I can't find her. So I called you. I was sure you'd know where she is."

"I don't know if Toni wants to see you again," Jill said hesitantly.

"She's not with someone else, is she?" came the worried voice at the other end of the line.

"No, but—" Jill began. She took a deep breath. "She was very shaken up by your leaving. Her whole life fell to pieces. I don't want to put her through more pain for nothing."

"But it wouldn't be for nothing, Jill," Brandt pleaded. "That's why I'm back. I can't get along without her. I've tried. I put all my energy into finding a job. I've been trying like crazy these past few weeks. I finally got an assistant director's job, starting in April, and I came up to see Toni and tell her. I know it will be hard, trying to carry on a long-distance relationship, but I'm willing to try it if she is. Won't you give me her number so I can tell her that, Jill?"

"I would if I could, Brandt," Jill said. "But I don't know where she lives either. Did you try calling her folks?"

"Nobody answered there. I tried calling three nights in a row. I called her old apartment, and they said she left several weeks ago. You mean she's lost touch with you, too? What if something has happened to her?"

"In a way something has, Brandt," Jill confessed. "In fact, I'm really worried about her." She went on to give him the whole story.

"I can't believe it," Brandt finally said. "Toni wouldn't join a bunch of weirdos. That's not like her at all. She must have been playing a joke on you, Jill."

"It was no joke, Brandt," Jill said. "After you left, she was really depressed, and then suddenly she started talking about new friends. I saw her myself, dressed in a long purple robe, walking along chanting and begging. And now she's out at that ranch on the weekends, and I'm sure she's scared and wants to get out."

"Then we have to get her out," Brandt said. "Listen, I've got a car here I've rented. I'll drive down right away, and we'll go out there tonight. This is the weekend so she should be there."

"That's wonderful, Brandt," Jill said. She felt as if a heavy load had been lifted from her shoulders. Brandt was daring and strong, and he would be able to rescue Toni if anyone could.

"See? What did I tell you?" Jill whispered. Shivering as much from fright as from the cold, she stood huddled close to Brandt beside the car on a lonely country road. The only sound was the wind sighing across wide, empty fields. Across a meadow, squares of light shone out of a lone building. The car's headlights outlined a barbed wire fence. "Look at the barbed wire," Jill pointed out. "Nobody could escape from that in a hurry."

"But there is a gate," Brandt said uneasily. "Why don't we just drive up to the front of the place and ask to speak to Toni?"

"Because they'll probably deny that she's here. And even if they would let us see her, I'm sure they wouldn't allow her to tell us her true feelings. They'd probably have guards in the room and make her say the lines they had prepared for her. Surprise is the only way, Brandt. If Toni suddenly sees both of us, we'll know if she wants to be rescued or not."

"So how do you propose to get in, if we don't

use the driveway?" Brandt asked, peering into the darkness.

"We'll leave the car here and use your coat to put over the barbed wire," Jill said.

"Thanks a lot," Brandt said dryly. "I happen to like my coat."

"Come on, Brandt. You help me over and then I'll help you."

"I feel kind of foolish," Brandt said as he finally managed to scramble over the fence. "Do you think this is really necessary?"

Jill glared at him. "If they were nice, normal people, would they put barbed wire over everything?" she asked. "Come on, let's get this over with. My heart is thumping so loudly I bet they can hear it in that barn."

She started to move silently along the edge of the drive. She was so scared that her legs would hardly move forward, but she forced herself to think of Toni waiting for help to come. They had covered only half the distance between the fence and the lighted windows when a huge black and white shape appeared out of the shadows. Jill stifled a scream and grabbed at Brandt.

"They're coming to get us," Jill whispered. Brandt put a restraining hand on her shoulder.

"It's okay. It's just a cow," he said. "I hope we've got the right place."

"At the gas station they said the Radlett place was just beyond the crossroads, and this is the first place beyond the crossroads. Anyway, we'll have a chance to look in the window before we do anything."

They crossed the last few yards to the old wooden building. As they got nearer, they could see light spilling out through wide cracks in the wall. They could also hear voices raised in anger. Jill crept up to the wall and put her eye to one of the cracks. The inside still looked like an old barn. Bales of hay lined the walls, and the floor was dirt. About twenty people sat in a circle on the ground. A young man stood in the middle of the circle, yelling angrily. As Jill watched, he pounced on someone at the edge of the group. Jill recognized the person instantly. It was Toni, who cowered back from the young man's raised arm. Jill forgot about Brandt. She forgot about danger. She rushed around the side of the barn, wrenched the door open, and burst in.

"Don't worry, Toni," she screamed. "We've come to rescue you."

Her remark didn't exactly produce the result she had expected. Twenty open-mouthed faces turned toward her. For a while nobody moved, then Toni asked cautiously, "Jill, what are you doing here?"

"I've come to set you free from all this," Jill announced dramatically. Her voice echoed through the big, empty barn.

"Oh, that was good, we could use that in the

play," the person standing over Toni said. There were muffled giggles.

Jill couldn't stand it any longer. She ran over to Toni and reached for her hand. "Come on, Toni," she begged. "Before they stop us. I saw that man raise his hand to hit you just now, so don't pretend everything is all right."

A grin replaced the stunned look on Toni's face. "We were only warming up," she said.

"Warming up? For what?" Jill stammered.

"It was an improvisation session, to get in character for our new play," Toni explained carefully.

Jill stared at Toni as if she were speaking an incomprehensible language. "A play?" she asked at last.

"Of course. What else would you expect a drama group to do except put on plays?"

Jill looked around the room at the be-wildered, half-amused faces. "You're trying to tell me this is a drama group?" she asked.

It was Toni's turn to look surprised. "What did you think it was?"

"A cult," Jill stammered. "I thought you had gotten yourself mixed up with a cult."

"A what?" Toni asked, starting to laugh. "You thought I'd gotten myself mixed up with a cult? Jill Gardner, have you gone out of your skull?"

"You thought we were a cult?" a boy asked.

"Hey, that's great. I like that. I'll be the Bhagwan or whatever." There was loud laughter. Jill's cheeks burned. "Well, how was I to know?" she stammered. "Your landlord said you'd joined a bunch of weirdos, and then I saw you all walking through the campus in those long robes, chanting and begging."

"You idiot," Toni said, shaking her head and trying not to laugh. "We were in costume. We had to wear those purple robes for the opening number of our show. Some of the guys even had on bald pieces. We walked across the campus on our way to the theater, raising money for famine relief."

"Then what are you doing out here?" Jill demanded. "I thought you'd been taken to the cult headquarters and were waiting to be rescued."

"You are a dope, sometimes," Toni said, smiling at her friend. "We've been lent this place for the summer, and we're going to do a melodrama out here. He's the villain, and I'm the heroine. That was why we were all so shocked when you burst in right now. We'd just been talking about having the hero come flying in from a beam to rescue me. We thought it would be great if he swept me up and—and—" Toni stopped speaking when she noticed a second figure standing quietly in the doorway. "What are you doing here?" she asked in a quavering voice. "Did Jill drag you here to rescue me, too?"

"Nobody dragged me, Toni," Brandt said. "I came looking for you."

"What for?" Toni demanded.

"Because I wanted to see you again."

"How was Hollywood?" Toni asked in a voice she couldn't control.

"Boring without you," he said. "Nothing made any sense without you, Toni." He started to walk slowly toward her. Toni stood for a moment as if she had turned to stone, then she ran across the room and flung herself into his arms.

"Boy, talk about a drama," a girl beside Jill commented.

At that moment another figure burst into the barn. "Jill, are you in here? Are you all right?" Jake yelled as he stood in the doorway. Again surprised faces stared at him. Jill ran to him. "Jake? How did you know I was here?" she asked.

"Are you okay? Is Toni okay?" he demanded.

"Everyone's fine," Jill said. "Everything's okay."

"I was worried sick about you," Jake said, gazing down at her as if the whole room contained nobody else. "Cassandra came to find me and said you'd left in a strange car. I remembered from the postcard where Toni was, and I guessed you had to be coming here. Then I found the empty car, outside the barbed wire."

"Yes, Toni," Jill said, turning to her friend. "How can you explain all the barbed wire?"

Toni started to giggle. "Cows," she said simply. "Mr. Radlett keeps cows in this field. He doesn't want them wandering all over the road." Jill started to giggle with her. Brandt joined in, and soon the whole room was rocking with laughter. Jake frowned down at Jill. "Would somebody please explain what's happening here?" he asked.

Jill flung her arms around his neck. "Nothing is happening," she said. "Everything is wonderful."

NINETEEN

"I still can't believe it," Toni said, shaking her head so that her blond curls danced. Toni, Brandt, Jake, and Jill sat together on bales of hay in the barn, drinking hot chocolate from a mismatched assortment of chipped mugs. "I cannot believe that Jill, my best friend Jill, the sane and calm Jill Gardner, would do such a crazy thing."

"I told you, I thought you were in danger," Jill said. Her emotions were stretched taut with the embarrassment, tension, and joy of the evening. "I was sure that the postcard was in code. You remember how you used to write me notes in opposites during school."

Toni laughed. "I do now," she said. "But I'd totally forgotten about it. I sent you a postcard because I thought you'd be reminded of Paris and the good times we had together, and you wouldn't be mad at me anymore."

Jill looked at her fondly. "I was never mad at you," she said. "Only scared for you. I really thought you'd be brainwashed and never let out again."

"You might have been crazy," Toni said. "But you were also very brave. If this had really been a bunch of cultists in the middle of a brainwashing session, you would have put yourself in a lot of danger bursting in the way you did. I'm really touched that you would risk so much for me."

Jill looked down at the steam curling from her mug. "You're my best friend," she said. "That's what best friends are for."

"I think that best friends must eventually start to grow to be like each other," Toni said, turning to Brandt, who was sitting close beside her. "I used to be the one who did all the crazy things, and she'd always have to rescue me."

Brandt smiled down at her tenderly. "You mean you've given up doing crazy things?" he asked.

"Of course," Toni said. "I am now totally mature and grown-up. No more embarrassing scenes with waiters in restaurants or flying over camera crews on skis. In fact, I've just realized how much I've grown up during these past few weeks. When you left for L.A., the whole world collapsed for me, but I've gradually built it back up again, and I've come to understand some important things. I've realized that you can't rely on just one person to be your support system in life. For years, I relied on Jill whenever anything went wrong. Then I had you, Brandt. But you both went away, and I had to learn to get along without you. I don't think I would have recovered so fast without my new friends here." She looked across at the sink where a few of the Purple People were turning dishwashing into a rowdy Marx Brothers routine. "They may be eccentric and unpredictable and eat out of cans, but they got me through a rough time, and I'll always be grateful to them for that. Now I've got a whole lot of friends who care about me. That's a good feeling."

Jake reached across and stroked Jill's hair. "Well, I hope Jill hasn't entirely taken over for you in the crazy antics department. I don't know if I can go through many more evenings like this one. I don't want my hair to turn gray before I'm twenty-two."

Jill smiled up at him. "I'll try to get back to my old, sensible self," she said. "Actually, the more I think about tonight, the more I don't know what came over me. I really did act just like Toni used to. I didn't think rationally at all. I just plunged ahead without getting any of the facts. That's just not like me."

"Does being in love scramble a sensible person's brains?" Toni asked with a little sideways smile.

Jill flushed slightly and smiled as she looked down at her drink. Jake slid his arm around her shoulder protectively.

"It's late," Jill said. "Maybe we should be getting back to Rosemont, Jake."

"And what about us, Toni?" Brandt asked. "Happy as I am to be with you, I don't want to stay in this drafty old barn any longer than I have to."

"I tend to agree with you," Toni said quietly. "This is a neat bunch of people, but this place is definitely not the Hilton, and I'm beginning to feel like I've had enough baked beans and canned spaghetti."

"I've got a great idea," Jake said suddenly, sitting up. "I have friends with a beach cottage on the coast. We could get there in an hour, and I know where they keep the key, just for spontaneous events like this one. How about a weekend away—all four of us?"

"That sounds like a terrific idea," Brandt said. "How about it, Toni?"

"Sounds great to me, too," Toni said, "as long as we eat real food."

"A gourmet restaurant nearby. My treat," Jake said.

"In that case, you've got my vote," Toni said.

176

"Offer me good food, and I'll be your slave for life."

Jake turned to look at Jill. "You're awfully quiet," he said. "Do you have to go to the center tomorrow?"

"No, tomorrow is free."

"Don't you think it's a good idea?"

"Oh, come on, Jill," Toni begged. "It'll be such fun—just the four of us. We all need to get away and relax."

"No, that's okay," Jake said quietly. "If Jill doesn't want to go, then I respect that. I'll just give you two directions on how to get there and find the key."

Jill turned and smiled shyly at Jake. "Who says I don't want to go?" she asked. "The new, improved Jill Gardner, who does crazy things without imagining all the possible dire consequences, definitely would not turn down a weekend at the beach with the people who are closest to her in the whole world."

"Jake, you are a genius," Jill said, stirring lazily upon his shoulder as they lay against a sun-warmed rock on the beach. "You've even managed the weather for us. It was freezing the entire week I was on the coast. And today we only need light coats."

Jake brushed the top of her head with his

lips. "Nothing's too good for my girl," he said. "You want California weather, you get California weather. Shall I call room service and have a few palm trees flown up to give you shade?"

Jill turned her face toward his. "You are truly nice, do you know that?" she asked tenderly. "You thought I was being dumb over Toni, and yet you still followed me, just in case I needed to be rescued myself."

Jake grinned. "I think it's time I told you something, Jill," he said. "Jake Randall is only an assumed identity. Underneath this shirt is another one with a big letter S on it." He reached down as if he were about to rip his shirt away, and Jill laughed.

"I do love you," she said, almost without thinking.

Jake's face was instantly serious. His eyes held hers. "Do you really, Jill?" he whispered.

Jill nodded. "I suppose I must," she said.

"That's good," Jake said. A wicked grin crossed his face. "Because I always need a few adoring women around to boost my ego!"

"Jake Randall!" Jill said, sitting up and turning to attack him. Jake laughed and wrapped her in an embrace. "Let me rephrase that answer," he said. He cleared his throat. "That's good, Jill," he said tenderly. "Because it makes the feeling mutual."

Jill sighed and lay back in his arms. "Everything's just perfect," she said at last. "The ocean is peaceful, and we're together, miles from any possible catastrophes. Toni and Brandt are back together, and life at Rosemont is under control. It's as if I've been working on a huge jigsaw puzzle all year. Sometimes I forced the wrong pieces to fit, sometimes I worked too fast, not stopping to study the whole picture. But now I feel as if I can really see how it all goes together. All the pieces are falling naturally into place—"

Jill's monologue was interrupted by a high-pitched shriek down the beach. Jill and Jake sat up in alarm in time to see Toni come flying around a large rock, pursued by an enormous sea lion.

"I thought he was a rock!" she yelled as she ran past them. "I threw my jacket onto him, and he woke up! I had no idea sea lions had such big teeth and could move so fast!"

Jill and Jake both started to laugh.

"What were you saying about life being peaceful, without catastrophes?" Jake asked Jill.

"I was wrong," Jill admitted. "I don't suppose life will ever be completely peaceful while Toni is around."

"Would you want it any other way?" Jake asked.

Jill shook her head, watching fondly as Toni ran up the steps to the cottage and the sea lion headed for the ocean. "Of course not," she said. "Toni will always be Toni, and she'll always get into impossible situations—in spite of her newly found maturity—and we'll always have our ups and downs, but we will never, ever get bored with each other."

Jake put his arm around Jill's shoulder. "You know, you are very lucky to have a friend like that," he said.

Jill smiled. "I know I am," she said. "I know she would have done exactly what I did if she thought I needed rescuing. She wouldn't have minded making a fool of herself or getting into danger, because she really cares about me, the way I care about her. I wouldn't trade that for anything—in spite of everything we manage to pull each other through!"

WINNERS

THIS EXCITING NEW SERIES IS ALL ABOUT THE THREE MOST ENVIED, IMITATED AND ADMIRED GIRLS IN MIDVALE HIGH SCHOOL: STACY HAR-COURT, GINA DAMONE AND TESS BELDING. THEY ARE WINNERS—GOLDEN GIRLS AND VARSITY CHEERLEADERS—YET NOT EVEN THEY CAN AVOID PROBLEMS WITH BOYFRIENDS, PARENTS, AND LIFE.

☐ **THE GIRL MOST LIKELY (WINNERS #1) 25323/$2.50**

Stacy Harcourt is the captain of the varsity cheerleading squad, but she wants to break from her rigid, boring image as "Miss Perfect." But in doing so will she lose the friendship of Gina and Tess and the captainship of the squad? Or will she realize that maybe her "perfect" life wasn't so bad after all.

☐ **THE ALL AMERICAN GIRL (WINNERS #2)25427/$2.25**

Gina Damone has problems keeping up socially with the other cheerlead-ers because of her immigrant parents old-world attitudes. But when she begins dating All-American Dex Grantham his breezy disregard for her parents' rules makes her question his sincerity.

☐ **THE GOOD LUCK GIRL (WINNERS #3)   25644/$2.25**

Cute, cuddly Tess Belding is the first student from Midvale's vocational-technical program ever to make the cheering squad, but she's going to be benched unless she can pass her French midterm!

Prices and availability subject to change without notice.

Special Offer
Buy a Bantam Book
for only 50¢.

Now you can order the exciting books you've been wanting to read straight from Bantam's latest listing of hundreds of titles. *And* this special offer gives you the opportunity to purchase a Bantam book for only 50¢. Here's how:

By ordering any five books at the regular price per order, you can also choose any other single book listed (up to $4.95 value) for only 50¢. Some restrictions do apply, so for further details send for Bantam's listing of titles today.

Just send us your name and address and we'll send you Bantam Book's SHOP AT HOME CATALOG!

Bantam Books presents a Super

Surprise

Two Great Sweet Dreams Special Editions

Get to know characters who are just like you and your friends . . . share the fun and excitement, the heartache and love that make their lives special.

☐ 25884-2 MY SECRET LOVE: Special Edition #1 by Janet Quin-Harkin. Laura Mitchell's mother has big plans for her future as a belle of Texas high society. But Laura's interests lie elsewhere, especially when she falls in love with Billy-Joe, a poor boy. So far she's managed to keep their love a secret, but when he's falsely accused of a crime, only Laura can clear his name. $2.95

☐ 26168-1 A CHANGE OF HEART Special Edition #2 by Susan Blake. Shy, pretty Hilary Malone has always lived in the shadow of her older sister Amy. Concentrating on her painting leads Hilary into a special friendship with Jason Wolf. But even Jason's love may not be enough to relieve Hilary's conscience when Amy is injured in a tragic accident. $2.95